THE CONTRACT

THE CONTRACT

DEREK JETER

with Paul Mantell

JETER CHILDREN'S
SIMON & SCHUSTER BOOKS FOR YOUNG READERS
New York London Toronto Sydney New Delhi

SIMON & SCHUSTER BOOKS FOR YOUNG READERS
An imprint of Simon & Schuster Children's Publishing Division
1230 Avenue of the Americas, New York, New York 10020
SIMON & SCHUSTER BOOKS FOR YOUNG READERS is a trademark
of Simon & Schuster, Inc.
For information about special discounts for bulk purchases, please contact
Simon & Schuster Special Sales at 1-866-506-1949 or
business@simonandschuster.com.
The Simon & Schuster Speakers Bureau can bring authors to your live event.
For more information or to book an event, contact the
Simon & Schuster Speakers Bureau at 1-866-248-3049 or visit our website at
www.simonspeakers.com.
The text for this book is set in Centennial.
Manufactured in the United States of America
0814 FFG
2 4 6 8 10 9 7 5 3 1
Library of Congress Cataloging-in-Publication Data
Jeter, Derek, 1974– author.
The contract / Derek Jeter ; with Paul Mantell. — First edition.
pages cm
Summary: In Kalamazoo, Michigan, eight-year-old Derek Jeter, who dreams
of playing for the New York Yankees, learns what it takes to be a champion on
and off the field.
ISBN 978-1-4814-2312-0 (hardcover) — ISBN 978-1-4814-2314-4 (eBook)
1. Jeter, Derek, 1974-—Childhood and youth—Juvenile fiction. [1. Jeter,
Derek, 1974-—Childhood and youth—Fiction. 2. Baseball—Fiction. 3. Goal
(Psychology)—Fiction. 4. Teamwork (Sports)—Fiction.] I. Mantell, Paul,
author. II. Title.
PZ7.J55319Co 2014
[Fic]—dc23
2014004045

FIRST
EDITION

*To my family. The life lessons you have
taught me, the examples you have set, and the
support you have provided have helped me achieve
more than I ever could have imagined.*

—D. J.

A Note About the Text

The rules of Little League followed in this book are the rules of the present day. There are six innings in each game. Every player on a Little League baseball team must play at least two innings of every game in the field and have at least one at bat. In any given contest, there is a limit on the number of pitches a pitcher can throw, in accordance with age. Pitchers who are eight years old are allowed a maximum of fifty pitches in a game, pitchers who are nine or ten years old are allowed seventy-five pitches per game, and pitchers who are eleven or twelve years old are allowed eighty-five pitches.

Dear Reader,

The Contract is a book based on some of my experiences growing up and playing baseball. While I worked hard on the field, I was encouraged by my parents to do my best off the field as well, in my schoolwork and in supporting my team and teammates and family.

I have tried to keep basic principles in mind as I work to achieve my dreams. The first is to Set Your Goals High. That is the theme of this book. I hope you enjoy it.

Derek Jeter

DEREK JETER'S 10 LIFE LESSONS

1. Set Your Goals High

2. Deal with Growing Pains

3. Find the Right Role Models

4. The World Isn't Always Fair

5. Don't Be Afraid to Fail

6. Have a Strong Supporting Cast

7. Be Serious but Have Fun

8. Think Before You Act

9. Be a Leader, Follow the Leader

10. Life Is a Daily Challenge

CONTENTS

Chapter One—A Dream Is Born 1

Chapter Two—All in the Family 13

Chapter Three—The Contract 22

Chapter Four—Practice Makes Perfect 31

Chapter Five—The Testing Ground 42

Chapter Six—Game On! 54

Chapter Seven—Stiff Competition 68

Chapter Eight—Play Ball! 76

Chapter Nine—The Mighty Yankees 86

Chapter Ten—Parents and Teachers 99

Chapter Eleven—Driven 106

Chapter Twelve—Wins and Losses 113

Chapter Thirteen—Checkmate 125

Chapter Fourteen—Winners 132

Chapter Fifteen—Field of Dreams 146

THE CONTRACT

Chapter One

A DREAM IS BORN

"Jeter, the rookie from Kalamazoo, takes a lead off second after his double. . . . There's a line single to right, Jeter comes around third, he's racing for the plate. . . . Here's the throw. . . . Derek Jeter slides under the tag and he is . . . SAFE! The Yankees win the World Series! Holy Cow! Derek Jeter, the kid who came out of nowhere, has helped the Bombers return to glory! Listen to that crowd roaring his name . . . Der-ek . . . Je-ter!"

"Derek! Derek Jeter! Are you with us?"

Derek's third-grade teacher, Ms. Wagner, was staring down at him, frowning. Behind her the whole class erupted in laughter. Derek woke from his daydream into an instant nightmare. He sat up straight and said, "I was listening, Ms. Wagner! I really was!"

"Well, then maybe you can repeat what I said—for anyone in the class who *wasn't* listening."

Yikes! He was really stuck now. What was he going to say? The awful truth was that his mind had been miles away—at Yankee Stadium for the Fall Classic, not here in Room 212 of Saint Augustine Elementary School in the middle of April.

Ms. Wagner's frown curled into a smile. Before Derek embarrassed himself any further, she added, "Never mind. This is an important assignment, class. So let me repeat it *again*, just so *everyone* gets it. Tonight's homework is a two-page essay entitled 'My Dreams for the Future.'"

A wave of giggling came from somewhere behind the teacher. For some reason a few of the students thought the topic was hilarious.

Ms. Wagner's smile morphed back into a frown. "I want you all to take this seriously, now. You have the whole weekend to think about it. Don't just write something silly—that you want to grow up to be Luke Skywalker or Tina Turner. I want to know your *real* dreams, the ones you could actually make come true."

"Ooo! Ooo!" Jamali Winston said, raising her hand and waving it frantically.

"Yes, Jamali?"

"What if we're not *sure* what we want to be?"

"You don't have to be sure about anything. This essay is your chance to think about your future and come up with some goals."

Derek wrote down the assignment, smiling. This was going to be easy! He knew what he wanted to be—a big-league baseball player. He'd wanted to be one ever since he was . . . well, even before he could remember.

The bell rang. Derek grabbed his things and stuffed them into his book bag. He threw on his coat. It was still pretty wintry in Kalamazoo, Michigan—which was not unusual for mid-April. Piles of leftover dirty snow were still on the ground from a blizzard they'd had two weeks before. And *more* snow showers were expected for tomorrow.

Derek sure hoped it got warmer soon, because Little League season was about to start. He sped down the hall toward the exit doors, dodging slower kids like he was running back a kickoff.

"Hey, Derek!" came a familiar voice from behind him. "Where are you running to?"

Derek turned and smiled. "Hey, Vijay. How's it going?" The two boys high-fived.

"Excellent, as always. Little League next week! You ready for some baseball?"

Vijay Patel had started playing ball with Derek and the other kids as soon as his family had moved into Mount Royal Townhouses. Vijay's parents were from India. They both loved cricket, but because Vijay had grown up here in the United States, he had become a big baseball fan.

The only problem was, he wasn't exactly a natural athlete. At first he hadn't been able to figure out which leg went forward when you threw the ball. Derek had helped him straighten that part out at least. From then on, Vijay had been his devoted friend, and Derek took pride in Vijay's improvement. On the night of the Little League tryouts in February, Derek had even given Vijay one of his Yankees sweatshirts so he wouldn't look so out of place—Vijay was wearing a jack-o'-lantern sweatshirt at the time.

"I sure hope we're on the same team," he told Derek as they got outside.

"Yeah, me too," Derek said, giving Vijay a pat on the shoulder. He meant it too. It was fun to have your friends on your team. But even more importantly, he wanted to be on a *really good* team for a change, a team that had kids with baseball talent.

Derek's last two teams hadn't done well at all. He had memorized all the ugly numbers. His Giants had finished 2–10 two years back. The following year his Indians had been only slightly better, at 3–9. He hadn't liked watching other teams celebrate at his team's expense, or the razzing he had gotten the next day at school.

The two boys walked back to Mount Royal Townhouses. It was a gigantic housing development with garden apartments, row houses, and a few taller apartment buildings. There were parking lots all around—lots of cement, and only a few green patches of grass and trees here and there. In fact, if it hadn't been for "The Hill," there would have been no large area of grass at all—no place to play baseball.

The Hill was really just a gradual slope, so it was *possible* to play there. But it was still far from ideal. Home plate was at the bottom of the slope, so Derek and his friends were always hitting and running uphill. Sometimes the outfielders tripped racing down the hill to make a catch, and wound up doing somersaults, or worse, scraping their knees.

They had to dodge trees, too! There were two trees in the outfield, and they often got in the way. But Derek didn't care. Any game of baseball was better than no game at all. His love of the game had inspired the rest of the players too.

Derek had been the ringleader of this bunch of ball-playing maniacs ever since his family had moved to Mount Royal. The kids had started calling it "Derek Jeter's Hill" in his honor—he practically lived there.

Every day, even in cold or rain, he'd be out there tossing a ball into the air by himself, until one of the other kids saw him through their window, grabbed a glove, and came out to join him. Two kids could play a pretend game on the hill, complete with radio announcing by Derek and whoever else was playing. If there were three kids, it made it even better.

With four or more kids they could actually play a real game—bending the rules, of course, but still, an actual game, with winners and losers and genuine thrills and chills. The games were often between the Tigers, the favorite team of most of the kids, and the Yankees, Derek's idols. Jack Morris versus Dave Winfield, Kirk Gibson versus Ron Guidry.

"Want to play some ball?" Vijay asked Derek as they came to the bottom of the hill. From here they had to go opposite ways.

"Gotta write my essay first," Derek said.

"You've got all weekend to do that!"

"Not me. I've got to finish *all* my homework before I get to do *anything* else," Derek said.

Vijay already knew that those were the rules in the Jeter house, but he shook his head, still unable to figure it out. "Okay. Whatever, I guess. See you later, then. *If* you finish before dark, that is."

"I'll be there," Derek promised. He already knew what he was going to write. At least, he *thought* he did.

"When I grow up," the essay began, "I want to be a big-league baseball player." Derek read it over silently. He nodded, satisfied.

A good first sentence, plain and simple and true. But that was *it*. That was all he had! What else was there to say about his life's biggest dream?

As he sat there thinking about it, his gaze drifted to the pin-striped Yankees uniform pinned to the wall. The back of the uniform was facing him. It had the number 31—just the number, not the last name of the player who wore it: Winfield. Dave Winfield. That was one of the great things about the Yankees. They didn't have names on the backs of their home uniforms because it was about the team, not the individual. For a minute Derek wondered what number he would wear if he were a Yankee. So many of them were already retired: 3, 4, 5, 7, 8, 15, 16 . . . Not much to choose from.

Derek was suddenly struck by a flash of genius. He wrote: "I want to play for the New York Yankees."

There. He read the essay over again, all two sentences of it, and decided it was just about perfect. In fact, it was even better, because now he had made it more specific.

What else could he add? Staring at the mostly empty page, he realized he had to fill it all with words—and another page besides. *I'm going to have to get even* more *specific*, he told himself.

His gaze wandered away again and found the big poster of Dave Winfield launching a long ball at Yankee Stadium.

Derek picked up his pencil. "I want to be the star of the Yankees of tomorrow, just like Dave Winfield is the star of the Yankees today."

Derek scrunched up his face. He knew something was missing. "Except I don't want to play in the outfield like

Dave Winfield. I want to be the shortstop instead." After another moment he inserted the word "starting" before "shortstop." *If you're going to dream, you might as well dream big.*

He continued writing, feeling inspired now. "I want to be like Dave Winfield, because he is a great athlete at many sports. He could have been a star in professional football or basketball, but he chose baseball instead. Baseball is my favorite sport too, even though I also play basketball and soccer."

He paused again. One page was almost completely full of writing. The empty second page did not scare him now. He knew he could fill it easily, by writing lots of facts about Dave Winfield and how great he was, and how Derek wanted to be just like him.

He read over what he'd written so far, and sat there, smiling. It wasn't like there was anything new about what he'd written. He'd had all those thoughts before. But somehow, there was magic in writing them down. Reading it now, he could see that he had put his life's dream into words and crystallized it so it was as clear as the blue sky outside.

He remembered Ms. Wagner's sly little smile as she'd handed out the assignment. Derek realized that this must be exactly what she'd been after! She wanted all the kids to think about their future—so that they would realize how important it was to pay more attention in class, and not talk or daydream so much . . . like he did.

When he finished the paper, he saw that there was still daylight, so he grabbed his mitt with the rubber band around it and the ball inside, and stuck a bat under his arm as he headed downstairs.

"Hi, Dad!" he called to his father as he crossed the living room.

His dad looked up from the term paper he was grading, peered at Derek over the top of his glasses, and said, "Did you finish all your homework?"

"Uh-huh. Two-page essay."

"Two pages, huh? And you finished it so fast?"

"Yeah. It was easy!"

Mr. Jeter's eyebrows arched in surprise. "Hmm. Well, I'll be glad to hear more about it later."

He turned back to his paper, and Derek headed out into the brisk late afternoon, toward the hill that was named after him. Just think what *else* they would name after him, he thought, once he was the starting shortstop for the New York Yankees!

Derek found himself in another daydream. There he was, in a real Yankees uniform, coming out of the dugout onto the big, beautiful diamond in the Bronx, hearing the fans cheer his name as he jogged out to short. . . .

It was a bit of a letdown to arrive at the rock they used as home plate, and to find Vijay and Jeff Jacobson waiting for him, instead of Dave Winfield and Willie Randolph.

"Hey, Derek!" Jeff said, high-fiving him. "Where you been?"

"Doing his homework, I told you," Vijay said, nudging Jeff. "You finished it fast, huh?"

"That's me," Derek joked. "The Flash."

"I'm gonna do mine Sunday night," Jeff said, waving the assignment away as if it were a mosquito. "I'm just gonna write about being a lawyer. My dad's one, and so's my mom, so . . ."

"A lawyer, huh?" Derek said. "That's cool. You'll look good in a suit and tie."

"Yeah, I'm gonna sue all kinds of people who annoy me. Like you guys."

That cracked them all up. Jeff had a wicked sense of humor.

"I would have written about being a doctor someday, and curing kids with cancer," said Vijay. "But luckily I'm not in your class, so I don't have to."

"Too bad," Derek said. "That would have been a good essay."

"What did you say you wanted to be, Derek?" Jeff prodded.

"What do you think?" Derek said. "A professional base-ball player."

Jeff snorted. "Ooo-kay . . ."

"Starting shortstop for the Yankees, in fact," Derek added, to make sure Jeff understood he'd really thought it out in detail.

"Ms. Wagner's not going to love that," Jeff said, cocking his head to one side.

Suddenly Derek felt nervous. "Why not?"

"*Come on*," Jeff said, snorting again. "Shortstop for the Yankees? Didn't you hear her say she wanted us to be realistic?"

"Why is that not realistic?" Vijay blurted out, before Derek could even react. "He's a good ballplayer, so why not?"

"Are you kidding?" Jeff said, laughing. "Give me a break. I mean, get real!"

Derek felt like he'd been punched in the stomach. Vijay put a hand on his shoulder and said, "You can so do it, Derek. Never mind what this fool here says." Turning to Jeff, he added, "Why do you say stupid things that only make people feel bad?"

Jeff made a face. "Oops! Sorry. Just sayin'." He shrugged, then seemed to remember something important. "Hey, by the way, speaking of the Yankees—I'm on the team!"

"Huh?" Vijay and Derek both said at once.

"*Little League?* Hello, didn't you guys get your notices in the mail?"

"Yeah," Vijay said. "I'm on the Tigers. That's good, huh? India? Bengal Tigers? Get it?"

Derek laughed, thinking what a great friend Vijay was. Somehow he'd helped Derek go from feeling lousy to laughing in about thirty seconds. And along the way, he'd stood up for Derek the way Derek had stood up for him.

"How 'bout you?" Jeff asked Derek. "What team are you on?"

Now it was Derek's turn to shrug. "I didn't get anything in the mail today. . . ."

"Uh-oh," Jeff said. "Sure hope they didn't forget all about you, dude. That would really stink, not being able to play." Seeing that Derek looked worried, he quickly added, "No, just kidding. You were one of the best kids at the tryouts. I'm sure the letter'll be in your mailbox tomorrow."

"I sure hope so."

"It *will* be!" Vijay proclaimed. "For sure, for sure! I hope you're on the Tigers too, Derek. That would be so cool!"

"Uh . . . yeah!" Derek said, still worried about not getting his notice in the mail. "Yeah, really cool. Hey, let's play some ball before it gets dark, huh?"

He started running up the hill, his heart racing and his gut churning. He couldn't wait for Jeff to hit him a ball so he could get his mind off all the troubling thoughts that were swirling in his brain.

Chapter Two

ALL IN THE FAMILY

At dinner Derek was still feeling troubled. He kept pretty quiet at the table, which wasn't like him at all. Everybody in the Jeter house always had lots to say.

Tonight though, it was little Sharlee who was doing most of the talking, while Derek was left to his own thoughts. ". . . and Miss Deena says I do the best pliés in the whole class!"

"She *did*?" asked Derek's mom. Her eyes widened so much, they were practically bugging out. "That's wonderful, Sharlee! You worked really, really hard on those, didn't you?"

"Uh-huh. I sure did!" Sharlee grinned. Even Derek, lost in his thoughts as he was, had to smile. Sharlee's joy and pride were infectious.

"And I told Miss Deena my brother's coming to the recital tomorrow," she said, nodding her head for emphasis and crossing her arms in front of her.

That got Derek's attention. "Me?"

Sharlee's four-year-old brow wrinkled, and her lower lip quivered. "You *are* coming . . . aren't you, Derek?"

"Um . . . sure I am!" He quickly covered up his surprise. "You think I wouldn't show up for my favorite little sister?"

Sharlee brightened instantly. "I'm your *only* little sister!"

"So what? You're still my favorite!"

To be honest, he'd forgotten all about the recital for Sharlee's ballet class. All those little kids had been working on their dances since the start of the new year, and Sharlee, the youngest ballerina of them all, had a solo!

There was no way Derek wasn't going to go. Of course, he *had* been looking forward to playing ball with the guys. . . .

"Of course he's coming!" Mr. Jeter said, patting his daughter's shoulder. "We're *all* coming. Our little girl's going to do us proud, aren't you, Sharlee?"

"Uh-huh!" she said, cracking them all up with her happy, confident attitude.

Derek wiped his mouth with his napkin and put it down. "May I be excused?"

"You may," said his mom. "You're awfully quiet tonight, old man. Everything okay?"

"I'm fine," Derek told her. "I've just . . . I've got some things to think about."

"Oh?" his dad said. "Care to talk about it?"

"Not right now, thanks," said Derek. "Maybe later."

Derek pushed back his chair, grabbed his plate and silverware, and took them to the sink. He gave them a quick rinse before going up to his room.

His parents gave him plenty of privacy all evening, sensing that something was on his mind and trusting that he'd tell them about it when he was good and ready.

Derek appreciated that about them. He knew kids whose parents wouldn't let them alone until they told them *everything* that was going on. Derek thought that often had a way of making things worse, not better.

That night he tossed and turned in bed, unable to sleep. Should he get up and tear up his essay? Write a new one about how he hoped one day to be a doctor?

It wouldn't be a *total* lie. On the few occasions when he ever thought about being anything other than a big-league ballplayer, "doctor" was often the job he came up with.

Doctors helped people; they saved lives; people depended on them. Derek liked that. He wanted to be someone people could depend on, one way or another.

He got up, switched his desk light on, and tried writing a few lines about being a doctor. But his heart wasn't in it.

The alarm clock told him it was past eleven. The house was dead quiet. Derek wondered if his parents were still awake.

He opened his bedroom door and glanced down the hallway. Their bedroom door was closed, but Derek could see light underneath it, so he figured it wasn't too late to bother them.

He padded down the hallway, staying superquiet so as not to wake Sharlee. She was a light sleeper and would wail if you startled her out of her dreams.

Derek knocked softly on his parents' door. Inside he heard stirring, so he turned the doorknob and let himself in. "Mom? Dad?"

His mother lay propped up in bed in her pajamas, a book on her lap. "Derek, honey, are you all right?"

Derek went over to her as she put down her book, forgetting to mark her place as she reached for him and hugged him. "Tell me what's bothering you," she said. Then, gently nudging her husband, she said, "Jeter! Wake up."

Mr. Jeter's eyes flickered open, and he raised his head off the pillow, squinting. "Oh. Hi, Derek. Something wrong?" In a moment he had gone from fast asleep to wide awake, and he was paying full attention.

"I have a problem," Derek said. "See, there's this essay . . ." And he began to tell them the whole story, from the elation he felt when the assignment had been given all the way up to the doubt he was feeling just that very minute.

At first he was afraid his parents would tell him to go back to sleep. But Mr. and Mrs. Jeter listened patiently, not interrupting as Derek poured out his dream of being the starting shortstop for the New York Yankees.

He told them how Jeff had reacted to it, and how Vijay had stuck up for him. He told them that he was thinking of changing his essay and writing about being a doctor. "Now I don't know what to do," he finished. "I guess I'll just . . . I don't know. . . ." He sighed, looking down at his folded hands as he sat on the edge of the bed.

By this time, his mom was sitting on his left and his dad had come around to sandwich him on his right. Each of them had an arm around him, and his mom nuzzled his wavy hair with her cheek.

"Derek," his mom said, "it's never a mistake to dream. Without dreams none of us would ever amount to much."

"I agree," said his dad. "It's up to you if you want to change your essay—but only if you're *really* going to change your *dream*."

"I'm not!" Derek said. "I want to be the Yankees' short-stop! More than anything."

"All right, then," Mr. Jeter said. "Let me ask you, old man—how hard are you willing to work to achieve your dream?"

"Really, really, REALLY hard!" Derek said. "I play ball every day, Dad! I'd play more if I could."

Mrs. Jeter chimed in. "The reason your father's asking

is because there's a big difference between dreams that are just fantasies and dreams you really plan to make come true."

"That's right, Derek," said his dad. "When your friend Jeff said you have to be realistic, he was right."

"He was?" Derek felt crushed for a moment, until he realized his dad wasn't finished talking.

"Yes, he was. Look, you're going to be starting Little League again soon. You know that most of those kids want to be major-league ballplayers. I know not all of them are writing their essays about it, but you have to understand, there are millions of kids out there right now, in every corner of the United States, who want to be big leaguers. I wanted to be one myself; you know that. If it hadn't been for my—"

"Jeter, Derek knows all about your college days," Mrs. Jeter said.

Indeed, Mr. Jeter liked to show his son the newspaper clipping he'd saved about the home run he hit while playing shortstop for Fisk University in Nashville, Tennessee. It was the only homer he hit in college, but he talked about it so often that Mrs. Jeter kidded him about breaking Roger Maris's single-season home run record of sixty-one.

Mr. Jeter cleared his throat. "Yes. That's right, Dot, I guess he does. In any case, you've got lots of competition, and plenty of those boys are great athletes. If you're going to beat them out for the job of your dreams, you're going to have to *outwork* them, right from the start. Understand?"

This was music to Derek's ears. He could scarcely believe his dad was taking his dream so seriously!

"Derek, you can do anything you want in life, if you work hard enough and stick with it," his mom added. "Right now you have to keep getting better at the game, every day—without neglecting your studies, your chores, your friends, or your family, of course."

"I know!" Derek said. "That's what I want to do!"

"Remember, later on it won't just be kids from Kalamazoo you're competing against," his dad said. "The closer you get to the ultimate goal, the tougher the competition's going to get. It'll be downright ferocious." He looked Derek square in the eyes. "Are you up for that kind of battle?"

Derek shot to his feet. "You bet I am, Dad!"

"In that case," his father said, "I think I can speak for both your mother and myself in saying we're right behind you, all the way."

"It's going to be tough," his mother added. "Really tough. But if you work harder than everyone else, and stick to it even when things get hard, we believe you can make it happen."

"Yesss!" Derek exulted, both fists in the air. Then he stopped himself. "So . . . you guys think I should hand my essay in as it is?"

"Why not?" his mom asked. "It's the truth, isn't it?"

"Now," said Mr. Jeter, "sit back down here. We're not

done yet. Before you go back to bed, we need to plan out your first steps. Every dream needs a plan to make it come true. And every plan needs a first step or two to get things going."

"So what might your first steps be, Derek?" his mom asked.

"Well, there's Little League, I guess," he replied.

"There you go!" said his father. "So what's your goal for this season?"

"To be the best shortstop in the whole league!" Derek answered automatically. "And to win the championship, of course."

"That's good," said his dad. "But remember, the team comes first. If it's just about you, you might as well play tennis or golf."

"So be the best shortstop you can be, and try to lead your team to a championship," Mrs. Jeter said.

Derek sat there on the bed, but he might as well have been sitting on a cloud. A half hour later, when all the questions he could think of had been answered, his parents finally chased him out of their room.

Derek floated back to his bed and got under the covers. His heart was full of love for his mom and dad, who hadn't ridiculed his fragile hopes and had even sworn to stand with him and help him achieve his goal.

And his head was full of stars, as he imagined himself being introduced in Yankee Stadium before the start of the World Series. . . . *"Starting at shortstop and batting second, number thirteen, Derek Jeter, number thirteen."* Yeah, that number hadn't been retired yet.

When he opened his eyes again, after a night full of beautiful dreams, it was morning, and the sun in a clear blue sky was shining directly on him.

Chapter Three
THE CONTRACT

"Can you believe this?" Derek shook his head as he stared at the image on the TV screen. "A *snow* delay?" He was wearing his Winfield shirt and Yankees hat, while his dad sat on the couch in a well-worn Tigers sweatshirt.

His dad looked up from the term paper he was writing and chuckled. "Hey, Detroit in April, you never know about the weather." Mr. Jeter was in graduate school, studying for a master's degree in social work so he could achieve his own dream—helping troubled teenagers cope with their problems.

The visiting Yankees were sitting in their dugout—that is, the few who hadn't gone into the clubhouse to get warm. One of the players who'd remained stood out—tall, muscular, with a huge smile spread over his face. He was stretching from side to side to keep himself loose. "Look at Dave Winfield," Derek said. "He's not inside staying warm. He's out there working, no matter what."

"That's the way to be," Mr. Jeter said without looking up from his work.

"He's a great person, too, Dad. Did you know he started his own charitable foundation to help kids?"

Mr. Jeter looked up again, interested—and proud that his son was using such lofty words. "A charitable foundation, huh?"

"Yup. He's the first active player to ever do that. When I'm the Yankees' shortstop, I'm going to be the second player to start a foundation to help kids."

"Okay. . . . I think that's a fine idea," his father said, smiling.

"Unless someone else does it in between," Derek said thoughtfully. "Then I might be the third . . . or the fourth."

"I see you're still serious about what we discussed last night," said his dad. "That's good. After you left our room, your mom and I jotted down some guidelines for you to follow. If you're going to be the Yankees' shortstop, you might as well get used to having a contract. Do you want to see what we wrote down?"

Derek nodded his head, then gulped as his father turned off the game and went upstairs. *What is this all about?* he thought. When his father came back downstairs, Mrs. Jeter was with him, and he had in his hand a sheet of yellow legal paper, which he placed on the table in front of Derek. Mr. and Mrs. Jeter sat down together with Derek. "No negotiating," his father said with a smile.

At the top of the paper, in capital letters, were the words *CONTRACT FOR DEREK JETER*. And below that was a list, which Mr. Jeter proceeded to read out loud:

1. Family Comes First. Attend our nightly dinner.
2. Be a Role Model for Sharlee. (She looks to you to model good behavior.)
3. Do Your Schoolwork and Maintain Good Grades (As or Bs).
4. Bedtime. Lights out at nine p.m. on school nights.
5. Do Your Chores. Take out the garbage, clean your room on weekends, and help with the dishes.
6. Respect Others. Be a good friend, classmate, and teammate. Listen to your teachers, coaches, and other adults.
7. Respect Yourself. Take good care of your body and your mind. Avoid alcohol and drugs. Surround yourself with positive friends with strong values.
8. Work Hard. You owe it to yourself and those around you to give your all. Do your best in everything that you do.

And below the list was this paragraph:

Failure to comply will result in the loss of playing sports and hanging out with friends. Extra-special rewards include attending a major-league baseball game, choosing a location for dinner, and selecting another event of your choice.

"Do you have any questions?" his father said.

Derek didn't know what to say at first. He thought he could live up to all the rules, but it was the reward at the end that really caught his attention. Maybe he would get to see the New York Yankees in person, and in the sunshine, instead of watching them on TV in the snow. "I think I can do this," he told his father.

With that, Mr. Jeter pointed to a section at the bottom of the contract that read, "I Agree."

"If you are ready commit to this, then sign here," he said.

Derek took a deep breath, picked up a pen, and signed his name with a flourish.

"We're both really proud of you, Derek," Mrs. Jeter said with a smile.

With that important discussion completed, Mr. Jeter reached back over to turn on the TV.

"Hey, look. The Yankees are ready to play!" Derek said.

"I don't know why you can't forget about the Yankees and become a Tigers fan like everyone else in this town," said his father.

"I'm a Yankees fan, like Grandma!" Derek said proudly. "Just because we moved here from New Jersey doesn't mean I'm going to switch teams. That would make me a traitor!"

"Well, I was never a Yankees fan even when we lived in New Jersey! Growing up, I liked the National League teams because back then they had more African-American players."

"Uh-uh-uh!" Mrs. Jeter said, and grabbed a gigantic bowl of popcorn from the other room. "No fighting in this house. Everybody gets to root for his or her own team."

Everyone laughed, and she sat down next to her husband on the couch.

"Derek, I'm happy to see you read and sign the contract. But remember, signing it is one thing. Living up to it is a different story."

Derek's attention, though, was on the TV screen. "Why'd we have to move to a place where baseball season is so short?" Derek complained. "If we lived in Florida, Little League probably would have started in February."

"Derek, you know we moved here for Dad's school," his mom said, taking his words more seriously than he'd meant them.

Derek's dad had been accepted by Western Michigan University as a master's student, so the whole family had moved to Kalamazoo from New Jersey.

They'd already lived here awhile, so Derek was used

to playing ball in the wind and the cold. And when it got too cold, he liked to practice his swing in the garage. But that didn't keep him from wishing they were someplace warmer, maybe in a neighborhood with a real field.

Sharlee came into the living room, wearing her tutu. A tiara was perched on top of her long, curly hair, securely pinned but leaning a little to the left. She had a smile on her face that made the rest of them laugh.

"Look! I'm a princess ballerina!" she crowed, spreading her arms wide and spinning around so they could get a good look at her. "Is it time yet?"

"Not yet, baby," said Mrs. Jeter. "Soon, though."

"Time for what?" Derek said, acting like he didn't know.

"Derek!" Sharlee cried. "My recital!"

"Oh! Yeah. I remember now." Derek laughed. "Just kidding, Sharlee. I didn't forget. And if I did, something tells me you'd remind me."

"But you're coming, aren't you?"

"Sure I am!"

By the end of the third inning, with the game still scoreless, it was time for them to go.

Derek had been checking out the window every few minutes all morning, to see if he could spot the mailman coming with his letter from Little League. Now he checked the mailbox on their way out, only to find that the box was still empty. Maybe they *had* forgotten him.

They all piled into the family car. Derek sure hoped the

letter was there by the time they came home—because practice started tomorrow, and if he didn't get a team assignment, what was he going to do?

The school gym was packed, with folding chairs from wall to wall filled with parents and other family members applauding the pint-size dancers on the stage.

Derek saw some of his friends there, in the role of older brother, watching their little sisters perform. Two of them, Jason Bradley and Harry Hicks, told him they were on the Yankees. They were really good players. With them and Jeff, the Yankees sure had the makings of a good team. Derek hoped he would be on the Yankees too, and not just because it was the name of his favorite team.

All the Jeters stood up and started applauding the minute Sharlee came onstage. At the end of her solo, Derek shouted, "Go, Sharlee!" which prompted giggles, and a "Shhh!" from his mother. But her eyes sparkled as she said it.

When the recital was over, Sharlee came out the stage door, where the families were waiting to greet the performers. She saw Derek, ran to him, and leapt into his arms.

He spun her around and said, "Bravo, Sis!"

"How was I?" she asked him point-blank. "Was I the best one?"

"You were fantastic!" Derek said.

"She was, wasn't she?" said Mr. Jeter, giving Sharlee a

kiss on the head that knocked her tiara loose.

She squirmed out of Derek's arms, bent down and grabbed it, and stuck it back on her head.

"You were awesome!" said Mrs. Jeter, clapping her hands. "Yay, Sharlee!"

"Derek," said Sharlee, putting her little hand in his as they walked to the car, "do you think I can be a ballerina someday?"

"Of course you can, Sharlee!" Derek thought back to what his parents had told him the night before. "You can do anything you dream of, if you're willing to work hard enough for it."

"Work? Hard?" Sharlee repeated, scrunching up her face. "That doesn't sound like much fun."

"It *can* be," Derek assured her. "Hey, don't you have fun when you're dancing?"

"Yes!"

"And it's the same with me and baseball. I don't mind working hard at that."

"But you work hard in school, too," she pointed out. "Don't you mind that?"

"Yeah, sometimes," he said, thinking back to the contract he'd just signed. "But I've still got to do it if I want to succeed." Then he gave her a look. "Hey," he said, "you're pretty smart for a four-year-old, you know that?"

"I know," said Sharlee, and that cracked them all up again.

Soon they were pulling into the parking spot outside their apartment. Derek raced over to the mailbox and opened it—and there was his letter! He tore it open and read:

Congratulations! You have been accepted into Westwood Little League for this season. You have been assigned to the Tigers with Coach Hank Kozlowski. Please be at Westwood Fields at 1 p.m. Sunday, April 20, for your first practice.

Derek's heart sank. He'd been hoping to play for the Yankees. And while he was glad that at least he'd gotten his team assignment, and that Vijay was on the team with him, he wondered whether he was going to be on another weak team.

Chapter Four

PRACTICE MAKES PERFECT

Derek's dad drove him over to Westwood Fields on Sunday a little before one p.m. There were actually four ball fields at Westwood. Each had its own chain-link backstop and fence down the first and third baselines. Behind these fences were the team benches. Farther from home plate, there were bleachers where family and friends could watch the games.

Since there were eight teams in the league, there could be four games at once. But only one team per field could practice at a time, so four teams were meeting now, and the other four would meet at three o'clock.

Team signs were hung from each field's backstop. Derek spotted the one that said TIGERS. "Let me out here, okay, Dad? I'll meet you over there."

After grabbing his mitt, he jogged across to the far side of the park, where he could make out Vijay playing catch with another kid—who threw the ball just like Vijay used to, with the wrong foot forward. Vijay was trying to show the kid which foot to lead with, just like Derek had taught him.

"This is my best friend, Derek!" Vijay said to the other kid. "Derek, this is Norman. Let's go, Tigers!"

Norman flashed a grin. "How you doin', man?"

"Good, good . . ."

"Vijay says we can't lose with you at shortstop!"

"Oh yeah? Well, um, uh . . ."

Derek looked around to see if he could find any other kids he knew and spotted Elliott Koppel. Elliott was just dropping an easy throw from a kid who looked like he couldn't be more than six years old.

Derek did see at least one kid who looked like a real gamer. He had a buzz cut and wore a Tigers jersey—from the real major-league Tigers. He was rearing back and firing fastballs into the catcher's mitt of Isaiah Martin. The mitt popped loudly with every catch.

Isaiah lived in Mount Royal Townhouses, too. He was shorter than Derek but about thirty pounds heavier. He had asthma and sometimes had trouble running the bases out on the Hill because he'd run out of breath. But he loved playing catcher, and he was a good one.

"Who's the kid with the arm?" Derek asked Vijay and Norman.

"That's the coach's son," Norman said. "Pete Kozlowski."

"He looks good," Derek said as Pete reared back and threw one so high that Isaiah couldn't pull it down.

"Maybe a little wild," Vijay said.

"He can hit, too!" Norman told them. "He was on my team last year, and we won the championship."

"He was on the Mets?"

"Yeah. He was our cleanup hitter. He had, like, a million home runs," Norman said excitedly. "We are so set!"

The Mets had crushed the Indians, Derek's team, 13–4. He didn't exactly remember Pete, though—probably because *all* the Mets had been hitting home runs that day.

A husky man in a baseball cap came over to Pete and put an arm around his shoulder. "That's Coach Kozlowski," Norman told them. "He coaches Pete every year."

Looking around, Derek saw his own dad settling down on the bleachers. He wished his dad could have been his coach. The problem was, while Mr. Jeter tried to attend as many practices and games as he could, he had a lot of other responsibilities as well. Not only was he taking courses for his master's, but he also was a student teacher at the university.

At home, Mr. Jeter always worked with Derek on his baseball skills, and he had promised Derek that as soon as he got his degree, he would start coaching Derek's Little League teams. But that wasn't going to help any this year.

Derek knew his mom would have been there too, but

she was with Sharlee at her friend's fourth birthday party. When Derek and Sharlee both had someplace important to be, their parents always played tag team. One time, their mom would go with Derek. The next time, it'd be his dad.

But his dad was his role model—the one who'd taught him to play baseball when Derek was just three years old. They had a secret arrangement: Derek would sometimes go outside and throw the ball against the wall of the house, getting ever closer to the aluminum siding. When—*bang!*—he hit the siding, that was his father's signal to come out and play with Derek.

Derek turned back to see Coach Kozlowski helping Pete with his pitching motion. He felt a wave of jealousy go through him.

As soon as enough kids had arrived, the coach called the roll to see who was there. He reeled off twelve names, but only ten of the kids were present. "Okay, team!" he said, tucking his clipboard under his arm and clapping his hands. "My name's Coach Kozlowski. A few of you know me from last season—Pete, of course . . . Ryan McDonough. . . . Um, I'm sorry. I'm forgetting your—"

"Norman," said Norman, looking disappointed. "Norman Nelson."

"Of course! Norman. Sorry. It's just . . ." He cleared his throat and changed the subject. "Anyway, right now all positions on this team are open. I'm gonna check out what you've got, and then we'll decide who plays and bats where. Okay? Let's start with each of you telling me where you'd *like* to play if you had your choice, or your second choice."

He started reading out names.

"Ernesto Alvarez."

"Pitcher."

"Second choice?"

"Third base."

"Okay. Chris Chang?"

"Shortstop, second base."

Derek looked over at Chris, the little skinny kid he'd seen before who looked like he was only six. Chris was wearing a huge glove that looked brand-new, like it had never been used. Maybe it was a Christmas gift, he thought, pounding his own, well-worn mitt.

Okay, so there was at least one other kid competing for Derek's position. Sizing Chris up, Derek thought that he could probably beat him out for the job. Of course, you never knew.

"Sims Osborne Jr.?"

"Third or first."

"All right. Derek Jeter?"

Derek looked straight at the coach and answered, "Shortstop."

"And your second choice?"

"Um, I really don't have one."

The coach seemed like he wanted to argue but didn't have time. He just shrugged, sighed, and said, "Okay. I'll just put 'no preference.'"

Derek wondered if he should have said something different. But it was too late; Coach Kozlowski had moved on to the next kid, and the next.

When Coach Kozlowski called his own son's name, Pete shot Derek a confident look that made him nervous—and said, "Shortstop."

Coach Kozlowski let out a little chuckle, said, "Surprise, surprise," and wrote it down on his list. "Okay, next . . ."

Derek couldn't believe it. The coach hadn't even asked Pete for his second choice!

"Ryan McDonough?"

"First base, pitcher."

"Okay. Norman Nelson?"

Maybe he just forgot to ask Pete for his second choice, Derek told himself. But it sure didn't seem like a good sign.

He'd thought all along that Pete would say "pitcher." After all, hadn't he just been pitching to Isaiah?

Derek felt like he'd been ambushed. Not only did he have real competition for shortstop, but the competition might already be over!

Two other kids had also picked shortstop as their preferred position. That made five out of ten kids, but the only one Derek was really worried about was Pete.

Coach Kozlowski sent them out into the field to one of their chosen positions, and he began to hit grounders and pop-ups to each of them in turn. He told them to field the ball and throw it back in to Isaiah, who was the only kid to pick catcher. He had always liked catching, and was the only one to bring a catcher's mitt and mask from home.

Derek fielded his three grounders and one pop-up cleanly and threw hard and accurately back to home plate. But none of the balls hit to him were difficult plays, where he could have had the chance to impress the coach. Anybody on the team could have caught any of those balls nine times out of ten.

Pete, on the other hand, got to show off his skills by diving for a ball to his right, getting up, and firing home so hard that Isaiah cried out in pain, took off his glove, and started shaking his hand out.

Pete laughed, then turned to Derek with a confident look and said, "Your turn."

Derek set his jaw and was all set to take another grounder and make a spectacular play on it, no matter what—but just then Coach Kozlowski said, "Okay. Everyone shift to their other choice of position!"

As the other kids switched positions, Derek just stood there at short. So did Pete.

Coach Kozlowski noticed that they were both still there,

along with Chris and two other kids who had yet to try out at short. "Pete and, uh . . ."

"Derek. Derek Jeter."

"Okay, Derek. You and Pete go over on the side there and take turns pitching to each other while I see what these other guys can do."

It was a way for the coach to avoid embarrassing anybody. Derek saw that, and he understood that it had been an awkward moment.

Pete grabbed a ball, and the two of them went into foul territory along the third baseline and started pitching it back and forth.

It soon became a contest to see who could throw harder and still throw a strike. Burnout, the kids called it. Both of them threw really hard, for sure. But neither of them threw too many strikes.

Still, after a few pitches their mitts were popping so loudly that everyone else stopped what they were doing and watched Derek and Pete go at it instead. His dad would be watching too, Derek knew.

Back and forth they went, blazing wild fastballs at each other, leaping and diving for the stray throws. Derek's glove hand stung, but he wasn't going to cry uncle. He gave back as good as he got, and he knew Pete's hand had to be hurting just as much.

In the end, neither one could claim a clear victory. Considering how wild they both were, Derek didn't think either of them would get to pitch anytime soon.

Luckily, three o'clock rolled around before Derek's arm totally fell off or his hand caught fire. Coach Kozlowski called the Tigers off the field just as the Yankees started to arrive for their practice.

Derek saw Jeff, Jason, and Harry—along with two other good players he knew, Skip Larsen and Jayquan Graves—all high-fiving one another. Derek couldn't help wishing he were on the Yankees too.

He tried to look on the bright side. There were five or six kids on the Tigers who might be pretty good. Himself, Pete for sure, Isaiah . . . That kid Ryan, the big lefty, was awesome at first base. Ernesto didn't throw hard like Derek or Pete, but at least he seemed like he could get the ball over the plate. And little Chris had good speed. *He'll steal a ton of bases,* Derek thought. *If he ever gets on base.*

Still, Derek couldn't help feeling disappointed as he watched the Yankees gather, looking like a team full of world-beaters.

"Okay, we're out of time, unfortunately," Coach Kozlowski said. "Next practice is tomorrow at four o'clock, right here. We'll do some hitting and some baserunning. For now, here are your uniforms."

He opened the top of a big garbage bag and started pulling uniform shirts out. They were green, with "Tigers" written in yellow script on the front.

Derek held his breath, hoping he would get number 13.

He'd worn it the past two seasons, and although it hadn't exactly proved to be a lucky number, 13 had been his dad's number in college. And his dad was Derek's original, all-time, and forever baseball role model (even though Dave Winfield was his current favorite).

Coach Kozlowski pulled out several jerseys and tossed them to kids one by one, based on who he thought would fit that size shirt. When Derek saw number 13 come out of the bag, he raised his hand and said, "Me! Me!"

"Sorry, Darren. This one's taken."

"It's *Derek*," said Vijay.

"Right. Sorry. I had a special request for this number." He gave Derek a wink, then tossed the shirt over to Pete, who quickly pulled it over his head.

"Yeah!" Pete said. "Lucky thirteen again, same as last year!"

"Here y'go, kid. This one should fit you pretty well." He tossed a different jersey over to Derek, who looked at it and made a face.

Number 2.

Pete was standing right next to him. He gave Derek a nudge and said softly, so that no one else could hear him, "Hey. Number two! As in *second best*!"

Derek tightened his jaw and pursed his lips so he wouldn't say what he wanted to say. Instead he shuffled off toward the bleachers, where his dad was waiting for him.

"How'd it go?" Mr. Jeter asked, putting his papers back into his briefcase. "You looked pretty good out there."

"Terrible," Derek said.

"Well, you were throwing a little wild. Try coming over the top more on your pitching motion. It'll help you be accurate. And make sure you follow through on your throws. Your hand should be pointing—"

"It's not that," Derek said. "I probably won't even get to play shortstop!"

Mr. Jeter looked surprised. "Is that what the coach said?"

"No, but his son wants to play there. And look, I didn't even get number thirteen."

"Well, two is a fine number."

"It's not thirteen," Derek said. "Speaking of which, guess who *did* get thirteen?"

"Oh." Mr. Jeter nodded slowly. "I see. Well, let's not get ahead of ourselves. You might still get to be shortstop."

Maybe, thought Derek. *But not likely.*

"And if not, just remember—that boy might be your rival, but he's also your teammate. Your team's not going anywhere if you don't all pull together in the same direction. Remember your contract? Respect others."

Derek knew his dad was right. But working together with Pete wasn't going to be so easy.

Chapter Five
THE TESTING GROUND

"It's the bottom of the sixth . . . last licks for the Tigers . . . and Jeter at the plate. . . . Here comes the pitch. . . . He hits it deeeeep to left! That ball is going . . . going . . . gone! That makes three homers for Jeter in this game. What a performance! We've got a future star in the making, folks!"

Derek sat in class, trying to keep his mind on the math drill they were doing. But it was almost impossible. His thoughts kept drifting back to yesterday's practice, and forward to the team's first game.

He tried to picture which kid would be playing what position—starting with himself at short, of course. Pete would be pitching . . . Isaiah catching, definitely . . . For sure Ryan would be playing first, unless he was pitching. But then, where would Pete go? . . .

"Derek? Earth to Derek . . ."

The wave of laughter from the class washed over Derek as he felt his cheeks reddening. Rats! Ms. Wagner had caught him daydreaming again.

"Sorry, Ms. Wagner. I was just . . . thinking about the assignment!"

"Oh really? That's interesting. Derek, because I was just about to give out the assignment."

Another wave of laughter. And above it Derek could hear the whiny, singsong voice of Gary Parnell, the class brainiac: "Come in, Derek. Do you read me, Derek?"

"I meant the *other* assignment," Derek explained. "The essay we just handed in."

Well, it wasn't exactly a lie. He *had* been thinking about baseball, hadn't he?

"Oh. I see. Well, that's fine, but try to stay with us. We're moving on to *math* now.'

Derek generally liked Ms. Wagner. Most times, she was a good teacher. But when she got annoyed, she sometimes had a sarcastic sense of humor that could really sting if you were on the wrong end of it.

"So, as I was about to say," she went on, "tonight's assignment is to study for our math test tomorrow."

Whoa!

Derek had forgotten all about the test. She'd mentioned it last week, he seemed to recall, but between the essay and Sharlee's recital and Little League practice, he'd been too busy to do any studying for it!

"There's nothing on the test we haven't already gone over. It covers chapters eight to eleven of your textbook. And it's all short answers. No essays this time, ha-ha."

Ms. Wagner smiled at her own little joke, which didn't get much laughter from the class—not like when she'd called Derek out for daydreaming, *again.*

Gary leaned over toward Derek and said under his breath, "I can't wait to ace this one." He meant the math test. Gary got all excited about tests of any kind, mainly because he almost always got the best grade in the class. It didn't seem to matter that he rarely studied. He seemed to understand math concepts before the class even learned them.

But nothing gave him more satisfaction than beating out the kid with the second-best grade. And that, most times, was Derek—especially in math, his favorite subject. Of course, it was Gary's favorite too.

The competition went both ways. Derek had always liked competing, at anything. It didn't matter whether it was baseball, some other sport, or even a test in school. And after the way Gary had just dissed him, Derek badly wanted to beat him on this math test!

Derek had been coming closer and closer lately. On the last test he'd gotten a 95. But of course Gary had beaten him again, with his third straight 97. The way Derek had been gaining ground, though, this test could have been the one where he knocked the "king" from his throne.

But now it was probably too late for that. With just one night left to study, Derek knew he would be hard-pressed to match his own 95, let alone top Gary for the best grade in class.

Every class had someone like Gary, someone who knew all the answers, and made sure you knew he knew. One of the worst things about Gary, though, was his attitude toward sports. "A complete waste of time," he would always say whenever Derek and his friends started talking about sports. "And in your case, Derek, a waste of a decent brain." Derek guessed that was his way of giving him a compliment.

But Derek knew he'd never get any real respect from Gary unless and until he beat him on a big test like the one coming up. Derek was determined to study like a maniac for this one, even if it was for only one night.

As soon as school was over, Derek pulled his uniform shirt out of his book bag and over his head. He jogged over to Westwood Fields, only to find that he was the first one there. He pulled his mitt out, undid the rubber band that kept the ball in the pocket, and started throwing the ball against the backstop.

Other members of the Tigers started appearing. All of

them were in uniform, and as they threw the ball around, warming up, Derek began to feel encouraged. They looked surprisingly better in uniform than they had in their street clothes—and they even seemed to *play* better than they had at the first practice.

Or maybe it was just his imagination playing tricks on him.

Coach Kozlowski showed up with Pete, each of them carrying a heavy duffel bag with bats, helmets, and catching gear. "Afternoon, gentlemen," the coach said. "A great day for baseball." Even though it wasn't.

Coach began by dividing the players into two groups for batting practice. Derek's group was at the plate first. Pete, as part of the group in the field, began the day at shortstop.

Derek grabbed a bat and warmed up with it while waiting his turn. He watched as Coach Kozlowski pitched to Derek's new teammates.

Half of them waved at easy pitches, or hit only dribblers and foul balls. And this was with the coach soft-tossing it, making it easy for them.

Derek tried to stay positive. After all, most of the better players were still out in the field, waiting for the two groups to switch.

Hey, wait a minute, he suddenly thought. He noticed that he was in the group that included most of the kids who were going to play in the outfield or sit on the bench most of the time.

Did that mean the coach thought he wasn't a good player? He shook off the horrible possibility, determined to show what he could do at the plate.

When it was his turn, he set his feet in the batter's box, just like his father had taught him, tapped his bat on the plate three times, and waggled it behind his right ear, waiting.

The first pitch came floating in. Derek swung so hard, he nearly came out of his shoes—and *missed*.

Breathe, he told himself. *Don't swing so hard. And watch the ball hit the bat!* It was almost as if he could hear his father's voice in his head, telling him to calm down, to relax, to do his best.

The next pitch came in high, and Derek reached up and tomahawked it. The ball nearly took the coach's head off as it rocketed past and then scooted between Pete and Chris, who was playing second base for the moment.

"Nice!" Coach said, pointing at Derek. "Way to go get it!"

Coach threw him another one, this time over the plate. Derek's eyes got as big as saucers, but he remembered to *keep* them open and not overswing. This time he hit a screaming line drive right at Pete, who ducked out of the way as it buzzed past his ear.

Take that! Derek thought, smiling. He hit the next two pitches hard on the ground.

On the last swing of his turn at bat, each hitter was supposed to run it out. Derek hit a fat pitch high and deep over the center fielder's head. He wasted no time showing everyone his speed around the bases. He'd always been the fastest kid at Mount Royal, as well as on his previous Little League teams.

Now he sped around first. As he passed second, he snuck a peek and saw the center fielder tossing the ball back in. But that wasn't going to stop Derek. He blew right by third base and headed straight for home!

With Coach Kozlowski shouting encouragement, Derek crossed the plate and leapt right onto the chain-link fence to stop his momentum.

Home run! Too bad it was only in practice. Still, the coach looked impressed. No one else in the first group of hitters had come close to belting a four-bagger.

Soon it was time for the groups to switch. "Derek," Coach Kozlowski called to him. "Second base."

Derek stopped in his tracks. Second base? "Um, I'm trying out for short," he reminded the coach.

"I know, but I've already seen you at short. I want to mix it up a little. I haven't decided anything yet. Nice hitting, by the way."

Derek felt crushed but did as he was told. He hoped Coach Kozlowski wasn't just jiving him about the shortstop position still being open. But Derek had a sinking feeling it was already a done deal and he was going to be stuck somewhere else for the whole season.

Pete took his turn at the plate. He didn't miss on a

single pitch, and everything he hit was hard, in the air, and to the outfield.

Derek stood there, waiting for a chance to show off his infield skills, but Pete wasn't giving him the chance. Finally, on his last swing, Pete hit a screamer to Derek's right.

Derek reacted in a split second, launching himself into the air and grabbing the ball in the netting of his mitt. When he landed on the ground, he set himself and fired a bullet to first, which got there just before Pete's foot hit the bag.

"Whoa! What a play!" Coach Kozlowski yelled, clapping his hands. "Yeah, Darren!"

"It's Derek!" Vijay called from home plate, where he was next up to bat.

"Right, right," Coach said. "Sorry. I'm not so great with names, but I'll get it sooner or later. Great play, though. I think we've got a ringer here, boys."

Derek felt a wave of joy go through him, and he couldn't keep himself from smiling at the compliment.

"Okay, Pete. Why don't you get back out to short," said the coach, once Pete had removed his batting helmet.

Derek's joy vanished in a split second. Why was Pete going back out to short instead of sitting on the bench while the rest of his group batted, like everybody else?

Pete played the rest of the practice at shortstop. He made a few errors, in addition to a couple of good plays. But every time he flubbed a grounder or threw wide of first base, his dad just said, "Okay, Petey. You'll get it next time," or something else encouraging like that.

Meanwhile, Derek was moved from second to third, to the outfield, to first—never getting another shot at his favored position. At the end of practice he asked the coach about it.

"I still haven't made up my mind about anything," Coach Kozlowski said. "I'll figure out the lineup at home, and you'll hear about it before the game on Wednesday, like everybody else. Meanwhile, be ready to play anywhere I put you.

"That goes for all of you kids, okay?" he added, raising his voice so they all could hear.

Derek collected his things and jogged over to his dad, who was waiting in the family car. Mrs. Jeter was in the front passenger seat, still in her business suit and her high-heeled shoes. Derek knew his dad must have just picked her up from her accounting job.

"So?" she asked Derek. "How'd it go?"

Derek sighed and shook his head. "To be honest with you, Mom, I don't have the slightest clue."

That was the thing. He really *didn't* have a clue about where he would be playing in the opener on Wednesday.

"I don't know how he expects us to practice our positions if he doesn't tell us where we're playing till game time," Derek complained at dinner.

"Well," said his dad, "you've got a point, Derek. But remember, it's always up to the coach. That's his job. Let him do his job, and you just do whatever job he gives you as best you can."

It was good advice, and Derek knew it. But it was one thing to *know* it was good advice, and another thing to *take* the advice. Besides, he didn't quite trust Coach Kozlowski. He'd seen other coaches favor their sons to the detriment of the team. He'd even seen one father yell "I got it" when he was coaching third and his son was at bat, so that the opposing third baseman would let the ball drop—which the third baseman did, much to the embarrassment of the coach's son. Some grown-ups had less sense than their kids.

All that evening, as he tried to study for his math test, Derek kept drifting back in his mind to Westwood Fields, trying to picture himself anywhere but shortstop—and failing. At one point he looked up at his alarm clock and saw that it was already nine o'clock! Bedtime, and he hadn't gotten through half the material he needed to review.

Derek closed his textbook, got washed up, and went to bed. In the Jeter house, there was no staying up after your bedtime—as referenced in the contract. If you couldn't sleep, you just lay there in the dark until you could.

It was after one in the morning when he finally shut his eyes for the night.

Derek had set his alarm for an hour early, so he could

finish studying. But when it went off, he was so tired from lack of sleep that he just hit the snooze button. He wound up getting up at his regular old time, still groggy. It was too late to do any more studying. He was just going to have to get by on what he remembered from the past few weeks of class.

Ms. Wagner started the morning by handing back their class essays. Derek took his excitedly, only to find, to his dismay, that she'd given him a B-minus!

"How did you do?" Gary asked him, eyeing Derek's paper. "B-minus, huh? Wow. That stinks for you." He held up his own essay—marked with an A-plus, naturally. Derek seethed as Gary turned away and took his seat.

Ms. Wagner said, "I just want to thank all of you—well, *most* of you—for your thoughtful responses to the essay question. I want to read out loud the list of everybody's dreams, because I think it's worth sharing." She cleared her throat and began:

"Maria Vasquez—nurse; Claibourne Preston III—investment banker; Josh O'Hanlon—attorney; LaShonda Martin—scientist . . ."

Derek waited for his name to be called, dreading the moment and the reaction he knew would come.

"Derek Jeter—starting shortstop for the New York Yankees." The class erupted in laughter, and Derek sank down low in his seat, staring at his desk.

"Simmer down, class," said Ms. Wagner, and she continued reading off their names and chosen occupations until she was done.

Derek didn't dare look up. He knew lots of kids were staring at him, laughing at his cherished dream. In that moment, he held on to the fact that at least his mom and dad believed in him. What did he care what anybody else said, if they were on his side?

"Now it's time for your math test," said the teacher, handing out test papers. "You have until ten thirty to finish and hand them in."

"Well, Mr. Yankees Shortstop," Gary said with a soft sniggering laugh, "I guess you're gonna knock this one out of the park, then, huh?" He waved his test in the air, chuckling to himself.

Derek set his jaw, grabbed his pencil, and went to work, determined to beat Gary on this test, no matter what!

Chapter Six
GAME ON!

"Okay, here we go." The Tigers were gathered around Coach Kozlowski in a tight huddle. Their green caps with the yellow bills were tilted back, and most of the kids were practically jumping up and down with excitement to get the game going. There were twelve of them now. Mark Feinberg and Sun Lee had showed up for the team's second practice, but neither of them seemed too experienced. Sun didn't even know many of the rules of the game.

The coach cleared his throat. "Leading off, and playing center field . . . Chris Chang."

Chris seemed happy that he was batting first, and Derek didn't blame him. Of course, Chris had asked to play either short or second, and he'd gotten neither one, but that didn't seem to bother him.

"Batting second, and playing second base . . . Derek Jeter."

Derek's heart sank. Second base?

"Batting third, at shortstop . . . Pete Kozlowski."

"Yessss!" said Pete, raising a clenched fist, then high-fiving every kid he could reach.

Derek turned away from the huddle and put a little distance between himself and the others. He didn't want them to see how disappointed he was.

"Batting fourth, at first base, Ryan McDonough. Fifth, and catching, Isaiah Martin . . ."

Turning toward the stands, Derek saw his father and Sharlee. They smiled at him and waved.

He waved back but couldn't manage a smile. He wished his mom were there, but she had to work till 5. She'd be there by the end of the game, but Derek wished she were there right now. He needed all the support he could get from the people who believed in him.

"Too bad, Derek," Vijay said, putting a hand on his shoulder. "You should have been the shortstop. The coach never gave you a chance."

"I don't know," Derek said. "Maybe he was right. Pete made better plays at short."

"Are you kidding? He also made a million errors!"

"Come on, Vijay, we're all a team," Derek reminded him, repeating the words his dad had said to him after that first practice. "Pete's on *our* side now. Hey, speaking of which—where are *you* playing?"

"Left out."

"Left field?"

"No. Left *out*. I'm a substitute. Coach said he'll put me in later."

"Oh, man. Sorry, Vijay."

"It's okay. Everybody has to get a chance. Nine places, twelve kids. My turn to sit down."

Derek laughed and shook his head. If Vijay could sit on the bench and cheer, who was he to complain about starting at second base instead of shortstop?

The Tigers batted first. Derek watched from the on-deck circle as the Indians' pitcher winged pitches right past little Chris. He probably would have walked if he hadn't kept swinging at pitches over his head or far off the plate.

One out, and Derek strode to the plate. He had his routine down, and he stuck with it now. He knew he had to calm down, to take a deep breath and make his heart beat a little more slowly, so that he didn't swing too hard and miss a ball he should be able to hit.

The first pitch came in, and Derek let it go by. "Strike one!" the umpire called.

"Way to look at one, Derek!" he heard his father call from the stands. "Now you've seen him!"

Derek nodded, and tapped the plate with his bat. Here

came the second pitch. It was halfway to home plate when Derek realized it was coming *right at him!*

He tried to spin out of the way, but the ball plunked him square in the left arm, halfway between his elbow and shoulder.

"OW!" Derek cried out in pain and collapsed to the ground, grabbing his arm where the ball had hit it. "Owww."

"Take your base!" the umpire said.

Derek got up and jogged down to first, fighting back tears. He didn't want to give the pitcher the satisfaction of seeing how badly he was hurting.

Standing at first, Derek tried to rub the pain out of his arm. He saw his father and Sharlee in the stands, concerned looks on their faces. His dad stood up, pointed to Derek, and mouthed, "You okay?"

Derek nodded, because even though he wasn't really okay, he was pretty sure nothing was broken and that he would be okay soon enough. His dad sat back down, patting Sharlee comfortingly on the shoulder.

Pete got into the batter's box and watched the first pitch. As soon as the ball crossed the plate, Derek took off for second base. He could hear everyone yelling, but he never looked up. He just kept on running until it was time to slide—his dad had taught him how when he was still in T-ball—and then down he went, kicking up a cloud of dirt.

"Safe!" the umpire called.

Derek looked up to see that the catcher had never even thrown the ball. Over the cheers of his teammates, he could hear his dad and Sharlee whooping it up. "Attaboy, Derek!" Mr. Jeter shouted.

He got up and dusted himself off. That was when he noticed that his arm had stopped hurting. *Nothing like a stolen base to take away the pain,* he thought with a grin.

Derek's steal of second base must have shaken the pitcher's confidence, because on the very next pitch Pete smacked a fastball way over the left fielder's head!

Derek motored easily around third and scored, while Pete, who wasn't exactly a speed demon, kept on chugging all the way around the bases. "Safe!" called the umpire as Pete slid under the catcher's tag.

All the Tigers let out a whoop, and Derek slapped Pete on the back along with the rest of them. They were teammates, after all, weren't they? Besides, the Tigers were now ahead, 2–0, with only one out, and it was still the top of the first inning!

Hey, Derek told himself, *maybe we can compete for a championship after all.*

Ryan walked and Isaiah singled, sending Ryan to third. Ernesto followed with another walk, loading the bases!

The whole team was standing in front of the bench, gripping and shaking the chain-link fence. The Tigers were already giddy with success, and it was only the first inning of the first game.

Alas, Sims popped up to second, and Elliott struck out swinging at a pitch that was nowhere near the plate. All the Tigers groaned. They'd had such a good start and gotten only two runs out of it.

Oh well, Derek thought. *I guess two runs is better than none.* He trotted out to second base for the bottom of the first.

When he got there, he saw Pete already at shortstop, acting like he owned the position. "Focus, Derek!" he heard his father call out. Immediately, Derek snapped to attention as if he'd had an electric shock. Forgetting all about Pete, he stared in at the hitter and got into his defensive crouch, ready for action.

"Hit it here," Derek muttered under his breath. "Hit it . . . right . . . here. . . ."

As if in answer to a prayer, the hitter whacked a sharp line drive over Derek's head. Derek leapt into the air, stretching his arm up as far as he could—and came down with the ball!

"Yeah! Attababy!" he heard Coach Kozlowski shout. "Woo-hoo! We've got ourselves a second baseman!"

Uh-oh, Derek thought. *Did I just mess up my chances of ever playing shortstop?*

The next batter hit a pop-up between third and short. Sims, who was at third, and Pete both called for it, and although it was a much easier play for Sims, Pete didn't back off. The two boys bumped into each other, and the ball dropped between them.

"I called it!" Pete yelled at Sims. "I'm the shortstop. I'm supposed to catch anything I call for!"

Taking advantage of the fact that Pete was busy yelling at Sims and paying no attention to him, the runner kept on going!

"Second base!" Derek yelled. He raced to the bag ahead of the runner, but by the time Pete picked up the ball, he had to rush the throw, and it went wide, bouncing into right field.

The runner kept on going. By the time Norman got to it in right field and threw home, it was way too late.

"Come *on*, you guys!" Pete complained, looking around at the rest of them. "Let's go!"

He said it like he was blaming the other kids for the mistakes. But it was Pete, not Sims, not Derek, not even Norman, who was to blame. What should have been an out had turned into an unearned run, all because Pete had made two errors on the play!

Luckily, Ernesto, the Tigers' pitcher, buckled down after that, striking out two of the next three hitters, and the Indians settled for just one run.

As the Tigers gathered at their bench, Derek watched to see if Coach Kozlowski would say anything to Pete about the way he'd yelled at his teammates. But the coach seemed not to have noticed his son's behavior, or if he had noticed, he had decided it wasn't worth mentioning to Pete.

Derek shook his head. If anybody needed a contract, it

was Pete. If that had been Derek yelling at his teammates, and if it had been *his* dad who was the coach? *Whoa.* Derek knew he would have gotten a real talking-to, one he wouldn't have forgotten for a long, long time.

But his dad *wasn't* the coach. And Pete's dad was. And that was the way it was going to be for the rest of the season. There wasn't a thing Derek could do to change it. He knew he would just have to find a way to deal with the cruel reality and make the best of it.

The Tigers' first two hitters grounded out, and Derek stepped up to the plate for his second at bat. He stood a little farther away from the plate this time, just in case another pitch strayed too far inside.

But the pitcher must have been thinking the same thing, because he threw outside on every pitch. Derek swung at the first one but couldn't reach it. He told himself to stay disciplined—it was what he knew his dad would have said—and refused to swing at anything that was clearly a ball.

Four pitches later he was on first with a walk.

Pete came to the plate again, taking practice swings that were so furious, Derek was afraid he would hurt himself. Pete's first-pitch swing was even harder—and he popped up meekly to the pitcher to end the inning.

Pete whacked the plate with his bat before heading back to the bench. Again, his father seemed to ignore his outburst.

Luckily, the Indians didn't appear to have a lot of great hitters. Ernesto didn't throw very fast, and he threw over the plate a lot. So while there weren't many walks, there should have been plenty of hits. But after the first inning, Ernesto held them hitless until the fourth.

But then, with two outs and the score still 2–1, Ernesto's arm seemed to get tired. He started missing the plate and walked two batters in a row. Then he grooved a pitch right over the plate, and the Indians' hitter whacked it deep to left, way over Elliott's head!

Elliott stood there, stunned, as if he didn't know what to do. Meanwhile, the center fielder, little Chris, used his speed to quickly run down the ball and throw it back in. Derek grabbed the relay and fired home just as the batter came barreling into Isaiah.

"OUT!" called the umpire as Isaiah held the ball up in his hand to show he still had it. Chris, Derek, and Isaiah had kept the third run from scoring, but both of the other runners had already come around ahead of the hitter to score on the play. The Indians were in the lead, 3–2.

Derek led off the fifth inning for the Tigers. This time he was determined to make contact, start a rally, and get his team right back into the lead.

The first pitch was over the plate, and Derek swung hard, smacking a sharp grounder to short. The shortstop was right there, but the ball was hit so hard, he couldn't field it cleanly, and Derek wound up with an infield single.

Well, it wasn't a home run, true, but at least he had his first hit of the season. And on the very next pitch he stole second base for the second time that day!

Pete proceeded to drive him in with a long triple to left to tie the game back up. Then Pete scored on a groundout by Ryan, putting the Tigers back in the lead, 4–3!

That was the way it stayed, until the Indians' last licks in the bottom of the sixth.

Derek knew that according to the rules of the Westwood Little League, every player had to play at least two innings in the field in every game. Coach Kozlowski had waited until the fifth to put in his subs, swapping Sun and Mark in as outfield replacements for Elliott and Norman.

Sun and Mark had been to only one of the team's practices. They seemed unsure of where they were supposed to be and what they were supposed to be doing out there. Derek now wished that the coach had put them in for the beginning of the game instead of the end.

As for Vijay, Derek was surprised to see Coach Kozlowski put him in at first base. Ryan was pitching now, and Ernesto had sat down along with Elliott and Norman.

The bottom of the inning started well. Ryan threw a lot harder than Ernesto, and he fanned the first batter. Two more outs, and the Tigers would notch their first victory!

But the next two hitters walked, and then the top of the Indians' order came to bat. On Ryan's second pitch, the hitter smacked a sharp grounder to Derek's left.

Derek made a neat play on it and pivoted to throw to second, where Pete had gone to cover the base. Pete took the throw for the second out of the inning, then fired to first, trying to complete the double play that would end the game . . .

Except he threw it on a bounce, and the ball hopped up and over Vijay's mitt! It bounced off the chain-link fence that protected the Indians' bench, and skittered into short right field!

Vijay quickly got to it, while Derek and all the Tigers started yelling, "Home! Home!"

Vijay threw, but his aim was off. Isaiah caught it too far from the plate to tag the runner. Now it was a tie game, and the winning run was standing on second base.

"How did you not catch that ball?" Pete yelled at Vijay, throwing his arms out wide. "You just cost us the game!"

Derek wanted to tell Pete how mean he was being, to tell Vijay to pay no attention.

But he didn't say any of that. They had a ball game to play, and he meant to make sure they didn't lose it. "Hey, we haven't lost yet!" he told both Pete and Vijay. "Let's go."

Ryan got two strikes on the next hitter. On the second strike, the runner took off for third. Isaiah reared back and fired over there.

"Safe!" yelled the umpire as Sims applied the tag a little too late.

"He was out!" Pete practically screamed.

"Play ball!" the umpire warned Pete.

On the next pitch, the batter hit a ground ball to Pete's right. Pete knocked it down, then grabbed it.

"First! First!" Derek yelled, seeing that the runner at third was already close to scoring.

Pete either didn't hear him or didn't listen. He threw home, and the play at the plate was not even close. "SAFE!" the umpire shouted.

And just like that, the ball game was over. They'd lost, 5–4. Their record was 0–1, and at least until the next game, they were tied for *last place in the league*!

Those were the thoughts in Derek's head when he saw, on the other end of the bench, Pete poking Vijay's chest, saying, "Do you realize you cost us this game?"

Derek went right over there. "Hey," he told Pete. "That's no way to treat a teammate."

"This kid can't even play," Pete said, giving Vijay a disgusted look. "Did you see that throw home? Pathetic."

"First of all, his name's not 'this kid.' It's Vijay."

"Whatever," said Pete as Vijay shot Derek a grateful smile.

"And second of all, it wasn't all his fault. Not nearly. I could name plenty of other kids who messed up."

"Are you saying *I* messed up?" Pete said, a challenging note in his voice.

"I'm saying a *lot* of us messed up. Including me." Derek

wanted to say something else, something a lot less nice, but he knew it wouldn't help the team win their next game.

"That's right, Jeter. Including you." Pete walked away, picked up the full duffel bag, and headed off toward his dad's car, where the coach had already popped the trunk.

"Thanks, Derek," Vijay said. "I hate that kid."

"Aw, he's just upset," Derek said. "Don't take it personally. It wasn't your fault we lost."

"He messed up at least twice himself," Vijay said, still feeling the sting of Pete's harsh words.

"I know it. He knows it too. He's just going to have to deal with it himself—and not take it out on other kids."

"Meaning *me*."

"You, or me, or anybody else," said Derek, although he knew he would never get into a real fight with Pete. Fighting never solved anything, and it could cost you plenty, not to mention the fact that Pete was way bigger and stronger.

Derek said good-bye to Vijay and went over to meet his family.

"Good game, old man," said his mom, kissing him on the forehead.

"Yay, Derek!" said Sharlee, hugging him around the waist.

That made Derek smile. He kissed her on top of the head. "Thanks, Sharlee."

"How's the arm?" asked his dad.

"Fine," Derek said, noticing for the first time in two hours that it still hurt, plenty.

"You didn't look too bad out there at second," said his dad. "Pretty good, in fact. Made some nice plays."

"Yeah, I guess."

As they got into the car, Derek saw Coach Kozlowski and Pete driving by on their way home. Pete was slamming the dashboard with his mitt, while his father just gripped the wheel and stared straight ahead, tight-jawed, stone-faced.

"Sheesh," Derek whispered under his breath. He sure would have hated to be Coach Kozlowski at that moment. He actually felt sorry for him, having to put up with Pete. He couldn't understand why Coach didn't just tell his son to quit it.

At the same time, while Derek would never have acted like such a baby, he understood how Pete felt. They both hated the fact that the Tigers had blown the game. Derek too wished he could be on a great team, a team that won almost every game.

And the Tigers did not look like that team.

Chapter Seven
STIFF COMPETITION

"'GATE.' Very good. Let's see, that's double word score . . . double letter on the *A*. . . . Twelve points." Derek's dad offered him the bag of Scrabble tiles to replace the ones he'd just laid out.

"Your turn," Derek said. He reached up to massage his left arm, which was still throbbing from the fastball that had hit it that afternoon.

"Did you ice that down?" his dad asked him.

"Nah, I'm all right."

"You sure? Ice is good for swelling. You might want to try it."

"Maybe later."

"Okay . . ." Mr. Jeter studied his rack of tiles, then laid

them out one by one in front of the word Derek had just made. "*I-N-V-E-S-T-I-GATE.* 'Investigate.' Let's see. That's fifty points for using all seven letters . . . plus two double letter scores . . ."

"*Dad,*" Derek moaned.

"Hey, it's not my fault I had such good letters," said Mr. Jeter, raising his arms in a gesture of helplessness.

"Two *I*s and a *V* are not good letters!" Derek pointed out, getting up from the table.

"Hey, where are you going?" his dad called after him as Derek left the living room for the kitchen.

"I'm going to get some ice!"

He made himself an ice pack and wrapped it around his left arm.

Though he had never come within thirty points of his dad, he still believed he could beat him if he just kept at it. Besides, as his father often pointed out, playing Scrabble certainly helped Derek's English grades. He'd been acing vocabulary and spelling tests ever since they'd started playing, back when Derek was in second grade.

He went into the living room and sat back down.

"See?" his dad said, smiling. "I told you ice would make it feel better."

"I guess." Derek sighed deeply. "I just don't feel like playing anymore, Dad."

"What's the matter? Too much losing for one day?"

Derek could tell his dad was just teasing him, and

usually Derek took it very well, giving back as good as he got. Today, though, he just wasn't in the mood.

"It's just not fair."

"Well, hey, I understand you're frustrated. So here's the way to get to where you can win." He lifted up the thick, heavy dictionary that lay on the nearby end table and handed it to Derek. "Just start with the letter *A* and keep reading."

"Dad, *it's not about Scrabble.*"

"Okay. You want to talk about it?"

"I hate being on a team where I don't get a chance to play shortstop!"

"Oh, so that's it. I had a feeling." Mr. Jeter took off his glasses. "You probably *would* make a better fit at short-stop than the coach's son. But that's how things sometimes go down in life. If you're going to make it all the way to the major leagues, you're going to have to accept some things not going your way."

"But—"

"Derek, I know it's not fair. But you've got to accept that it's the *coach's decision.* You may not like it, but you've got to abide by it, and *respect* it. Even if he's doing it to keep peace at home."

"Then why aren't *you* the coach?"

Derek could feel a stinging sensation as his eyes welled up with tears. He turned and ran straight upstairs to his room, without waiting for an answer. He threw himself facedown on his bed, feeling horrible.

He knew what came next, too. His dad would be coming up the stairs any minute.

But instead of his dad's footsteps, he heard the front door open downstairs and his mother's cheerful voice. His father's reply was muffled, and Derek couldn't make any of it out, but right away his mom's voice got less cheerful, softer, more concerned.

When Derek finally heard footsteps coming up the stairs, they were his mom's, not his dad's. "You want to tell me about it?" she asked, standing in the doorway.

"Not really," said Derek, staring at the mattress.

She came into the room and sat down on the side of the bed, patting Derek gently on the shoulder. "It's okay to get frustrated, old man. None of us would ever make big changes in our lives if we didn't get frustrated sometimes. We just have to turn that frustration into determination."

"But it's so . . ."

"Unfair?"

"Yes! Why can't Dad be the coach?"

"Derek, you know the answer to that question. We've talked about it a hundred times. Your dad wants very much to be your coach. Don't you think he feels bad about all of this?"

"If he were the coach, I'd be the shortstop for sure!"

"If he were the coach, he'd do whatever he thought was best for the team, and of course for you. But he's working very hard right now . . ."

"I know."

". . . teaching, and taking courses for his master's degree . . ."

"I know, but—"

"Derek, remember the other night, when we talked about your life's dream?"

"Uh-huh."

"Well, your dad has a life's dream too—to help kids and teens get their lives back on track. I know he's grateful and glad that you've got a dream, and that you're following it. He knows you can't go wrong shooting for your dream, as long as it's a good one."

Derek stayed silent, taking it all in. He felt bad because he knew he'd been acting selfishly. He knew he had probably hurt his dad's feelings by what he'd said about him not being the coach. He wished now that he'd never said that, but he knew it was too late to take it back.

His mom must have been reading his mind, because she said, "It's okay to feel however you feel, Derek. It's what we *say* and *do* that counts. I know, and your dad knows, that you're going to figure all this out in a good way. Just stick to your big dream, and you'll find a way through all the little stuff."

After kissing him on the forehead, she left the room, to give him time and space to work things out. One thing was for sure—from here on in, he was going to make extra sure he acted in a way to make both his parents proud.

He realized how proud he was of them, and how lucky he and Sharlee were. What was rule number one on the contract? "Family comes first."

His parents had met in Germany when they were both in the army, and they had fallen in love despite their different backgrounds. His father was raised by a single mother in Alabama, and he was determined to be the kind of father he never knew. Derek's mother grew up in a close-knit New Jersey family, and together she and Derek's father navigated a world that didn't exactly welcome interracial couples.

Derek's problems suddenly didn't seem that big.

"We beat the Phillies 10–0!" Jeff whispered, loud enough for every kid in the back of the class to hear, but not quite loud enough to attract the attention of Ms. Wagner, who was explaining a math problem while writing on the blackboard.

Jeff had worn his Yankees uniform shirt to school that day—number 13, Derek noticed, green with envy. "They had to call the mercy rule!"

"What's the mercy rule?" Gary asked, clueless.

Derek tried to explain. "It's when one team is beating the other so bad—"

"Ten runs or more," Jeff interrupted.

"So badly that they call off the rest of the game so the losers don't feel too crushed," Derek finished.

"Doesn't sound too merciful to me," Gary decided. "Besides, if you ask me, anyone who wastes their time on sports is already a loser."

"Aw, what do you know?" Jeff waved him off. "How'd your team do, Derek? Did you win?"

"Nah. We should have, but we blew it. We had a—"

"Derek Jeter!" Ms. Wagner called. "Are you following the lesson, or do you and your friends need a conversation break?"

The whole class laughed—even Jeff and Gary. Just his luck that *he'd* been the one talking when she'd turned around and noticed.

"No, Ms. Wagner. Sorry," he said.

"All right, then. Let's move forward," she said, wiping the chalk dust off her hands. "Now, class. Be quiet and pay attention. I have your math tests here."

She took a pile of papers off her desk and started passing them out. "Most of you did well, a few of you need to hit the books a little harder . . ."

Derek took the paper she handed him, and stared in disbelief at the mark he'd gotten—*84*! He couldn't believe it. He hadn't gotten less than a 90 on a math test all year!

He thought back to that last day of studying, when he hadn't been able to concentrate because his mind had kept wandering back to his problems with his Little League team. How had he let this happen? It might have been an okay grade for somebody else, but to Derek an 84 on a math test—any test—was a disaster!

He knew his parents would feel the same way. That's why focusing on schoolwork was in the contract, and now he had already broken it. They expected the best from him, and he usually delivered. This time he'd fallen way short of what he expected of himself. Forget about beating out Gary. He hadn't come close to his own usual high grades!

Gary came over to brag. "Ninety-seven! Fourth time in a row!" he said, waving his test in Derek's face. "How'd *you* do, Mr. Yankees Shortstop?"

Shaking his head and staring down at his desk, Derek took his hand off the paper to reveal the horrifying truth.

"Eighty-four! Whoa. That stinks, even for you!" Gary said, faking sympathy. "Hey, maybe you should study more, instead of wasting all your time playing sports?"

Derek had no answer for him. But he was seething inside. Somehow, even if he had to study until his eyes crossed, he was going to beat Gary Parnell on their next math test!

Chapter Eight
PLAY BALL!

Coach Kozlowski's lineup for the Tigers' second game—against the Mets—was the same as for their opener. Derek was at second base, batting second. He didn't like it, but he wasn't thinking about that today. He was thinking about winning a ball game.

The Tigers were the "visiting" team again, which really only meant they batted first, since all the kids were from the same part of town. Chris led off with a walk.

Derek came to the plate next. He couldn't wait to get a swing at the ball, but he remembered what his dad had told him: "Take the first pitch from a pitcher you haven't seen before, just to get an idea of what kind of stuff he has."

He watched the first pitch go by for a strike. As soon as the catcher caught it, Chris took off for second base. His steal attempt caught the catcher by surprise, and his late throw to second was off, ending up in center field.

Chris wound up on third, and Derek smelled a run batted in for the taking.

The next pitch was in the dirt. Another fastball, but unlike the first one, it was easy for Derek to let this one go by. Not too fast for him to catch up with, he noted, digging into the batter's box.

The third pitch was right down the middle.

Derek swung so hard, his feet left the ground. He barely hit the ball off the end of the bat. Luckily, it skittered down the first baseline, right between the first baseman and the bag. "Fair ball!" the umpire called.

Chris scored, and Derek wound up on second with a squib double. He clapped his hands together so hard it hurt, but he didn't care. "That's what I'm talkin' about!" he yelled to himself.

Pete came to the plate. With the first pitch, Derek was on his way to third. "Safe!" called the umpire. Derek got up and dusted himself off. He could hear Coach clapping and saying, "Automatic!" meaning that anytime Derek got on base, he was going to steal successfully. To this point in the season, it had been true.

In fact, so far Derek was the hero of the game—but not for long. He was about to give way to an even bigger hero.

Pete took the next pitch way deep, and there was no doubt about this one. He jogged around the bases while Derek stood on home plate, waiting to high-five him. 3–0, Tigers!

These Mets were obviously not the previous year's championship version. Still, three runs was all the Tigers got that inning, in spite of a double by Ernesto. And in the bottom of the first, the Tigers gave the lead right back.

Pete started the damage by muffing an easy grounder. He had it in his mitt but lost control of the ball when taking it out to throw it. "Arrrghhh!" he groaned, covering his head with his mitt. But this time, there was no one to blame but himself.

Ernesto didn't seem to have his best stuff on the mound. He walked two hitters to load the bases, and even though he got the next two on strikeouts, he gave up a three-run double before getting out of the inning.

Derek doubled again with two outs in the second, scoring Norman, who'd walked ahead of him. Norman whooped it up, deliriously happy, when he crossed the plate. "That's my first run scored!" Derek heard him saying. "EVER!"

Derek felt happy for him, all the more so because *he* was the one who'd driven Norman in. He hoped he could do it again this season, for every one of those kids on the Tigers who'd never scored a run in a real Little League game.

Pete came up again, waggling his bat, glaring at the

pitcher as though he were ready to knock his head off. Derek tried to distract the pitcher, who paid no attention because he was so intimidated by Pete.

The pitcher threw him a big fat fastball—and Pete swung right through it. Derek shook his head. *Pete might have hit that one if he hadn't closed his eyes,* he thought.

On the next pitch Derek took matters into his own hands, breaking for third. He made it easily, and as he got up, he heard his teammates chanting his name. "Der-ek! Der-ek!"

Pete singled on the next pitch, and the Tigers were up 5–3. Derek came back to the bench and high-fived his teammates. But now the Tigers were chanting, "Pete! Pete! Pete!"

"Yo, Pete! You're the man!" Chris shouted out. "Woo-hoo!"

"Go, Pete!" Isaiah echoed.

"Yeah, Pete!" Coach added his voice to the chorus.

Ryan hit a grounder to second to end the inning, but at least the Tigers were up.

After his poor first inning, Ernesto struck out the side in the second, third, and fourth. Ryan replaced him in the fifth and allowed only one hit. But in all that time the Tigers didn't score either. In the sixth, Derek hit a screaming line drive that made the second baseman duck for cover.

Derek stopped at first when the right fielder made a

good throw into second, but he took second on the next pitch, when the ball got past the catcher. Then Pete smacked another homer, and the Tigers went up by four runs, 7–3!

All they had to do now was hold on to their lead. But the Mets weren't giving up, and rallied in the bottom of the inning, loading the bases with two out. Then their cleanup hitter hit a line drive to Pete's left. He leapt into the air and made a great play to knock it down. All Pete would have had to do was hold on to the ball—only one run would have scored. But he tried to make a spectacular play at first. He had no chance of catching the runner, even if the throw had been on target. But it wasn't. It went off into right field, and two more runs scored!

The tying run was now on third. Ryan reared back and threw his best fastball. The hitter swung, and lofted a pop-up just to Derek's right.

"I got it! I got it!" he yelled.

He heard Pete saying "I got it!" too. Derek knew the ball was to the right of the bag, and so should have been the second baseman's ball. But Derek also knew it was the shortstop's call, as captain of the infield. So he backed off, saying, "Take it! Take it!"

And Pete did—with both hands, just to make sure. The game ended with the Tigers up, 7–6.

As happy as Derek was that they'd managed to save the victory, he was annoyed by the way the whole team mobbed Pete—their hero—forgetting that Pete was the one who'd committed two key errors that had almost cost them the game.

Pete was loving it, doing a little victory dance until his dad lined them all up for the traditional postgame handshake with the opposing team.

Oh well, thought Derek. *At least there won't be any tantrums this week.*

Because he'd gone straight from school to the game, it was only afterward that Derek remembered the math test and his embarrassing grade on it.

He'd mentioned the test to his parents beforehand, and he knew they never forgot anything he told them, especially about schoolwork. So it was clearly just a matter of time before one of them asked him how it had gone.

"So, how'd it go today?" His mom was setting a casserole down in the center of the table before sitting down herself.

"We won," Derek said innocently, but he knew what she meant.

"The math test," she said. "How'd you do?"

Well, that didn't take long, Derek thought. He sighed and shook his head. "Not too well."

"Really?" His father stopped cutting the casserole into squares and looked up at him. "Not too well, as in . . ."

"As in eighty-four." Derek sighed again.

"What?" It came from both his parents at the same time.

While 84 might have been an okay grade, or even a good one, for some kids, it wasn't for Derek. Math had always been his best subject in school, right from the beginning.

"Uh-oh," said Sharlee, covering her head and grimacing. If she'd thought it would make the rest of them laugh, she'd been mistaken.

"Why do you think you didn't do better?" his mom asked.

Derek shrugged. "She gave us the assignment a week before, but I guess I forgot about it until she reminded us. That was the day before the test. and I couldn't concentrate that night."

"Because you were too worried about baseball." His dad said it like it was a fact, not a question.

"I guess," Derek admitted. "But I couldn't help it! Little League was about to start, and I was worried—"

"We know all about it," his dad said. "But—"

"I know, I know," Derek said, hoping to avoid any more criticism. "Rule number two."

"Derek," said his mom, putting a hand on his arm, "there's no excuse. You always have to work your hardest if you want to achieve your dream."

"I know, Mom," Derek said, "but *sports* is my dream!"

"I know," said Mrs. Jeter. "But you can't do it at the expense of schoolwork."

"Doing well in school is the ticket that gets you into the ballpark, and into the game!" his dad added. "Where would

I be today if I hadn't gotten that college scholarship?"

"You got a *baseball* scholarship, Dad," Derek pointed out.

"But I needed good grades to get it!" Mr. Jeter insisted. "And I had to keep up my good grades all through college to keep getting my scholarship money!"

"Don't you see, old man?" his mom said. "You can't let yourself get distracted. It's not one thing or the other. You've got a very big dream, and to make it happen, you're going to have to do your best. All the time, not some of the time. If doing your best isn't a habit, you won't be able to call on that when you need it most."

"That's right," his dad said. "Don't worry. You'll always find time to practice doing the thing you love, so try to love what you have to do. And doing well in school will make you smarter, too. You're going to find out someday that being smart pays off, even on the ball field. *Especially* on the ball field!"

"How's that?" Derek wondered.

"Even if you're playing against players who are better than you—better hitters, better fielders, whatever—you can always get an edge by outworking them *and* by *out-thinking* them."

"Like . . . math?" Derek didn't quite get it.

"Hey, there's a lot of math in baseball!" his mom said, clapping him on the shoulder.

"There is?"

"Sure!" she said. "I'm an accountant, right? So I definitely know what I'm talking about!"

"For instance?"

"For instance, how many times have you been up at bat this season?"

"Uh . . . six? No, seven."

"See? Already, we've got a number!" she said, rubbing her hands together enthusiastically. "Now, how many times did you make an out?"

"Once."

"You got how many hits?"

"Four. Plus I walked once and was hit by that pitch."

"Right, right," she said. "How's your arm, by the way?"

"It feels fine now, thanks. So, where are you going with this?" He was curious now, for sure.

"So since walks and getting hit by a pitch don't count as at bats, you are batting .800!"

"Eight hundred percent?" Derek said, scrunching up his face. "How's that possible?"

"Not percent. It would be eighty percent, actually. It's point eight, zero, zero. At any rate, it's a really good batting average—and it's math!"

"I've got to admit, that's pretty cool," Derek said, grinning. He was batting .800! Sure, it was only two games, but it was something to be proud of and happy about!

"Don't think you're always going to bat .800," his dad warned. "You've got a pretty good swing, and a nice approach at the plate, but nobody stays that good for long in the game of baseball. Batting .300 in the pros will give you a good shot at the Hall of Fame. If you're dreaming of being a pro, you'd better realize that right now."

After dinner, Derek headed straight toward the stairs to go to his room.

"You okay?" his mom wondered as she saw him go.

"I'm fine! Gonna do some math."

"Great! Just checking."

He ran upstairs and got out a pencil and paper.

Derek knew he might never get to play shortstop for the Tigers that season. But there was one thing that *was* in his power to make happen.

Come whatever, he was going to outscore Gary on their next math test!

Chapter Nine

THE MIGHTY YANKEES

Winter finally turned to spring in Kalamazoo. The snow piles were now puddles. Flowers and buds came out on all the trees and bushes. Kids shed their coats and went around in sweaters or just their shirts.

And, incredibly, the Tigers won their next two games! They beat a terrible Marlins team, 16–13. Then they beat the Dodgers, who were even worse, with a score of 18–9.

Both of those games took a long time because there were so many walks, hits, and runs scored by both sides. The Tigers were hitting weak pitchers well, but they weren't getting any better out in the field. Pete continued to make errors, and so did everybody else. Even Derek muffed a grounder once, ruining his perfect fielding percentage. The thing was, nobody on the team seemed to notice that Pete was playing poorly at short, because they were making just as many errors.

The main thing keeping the Tigers happy was that they were winning. And they were winning because they were hitting. Boy, were they hitting! Pete had six homers in their first four games. But he wasn't the only one. Ryan, Sims, and Isaiah all had homers. Chris was getting hits that became doubles because he was so fast. Even Vijay got a single, after which he did a little dance of triumph on the first-base bag!

Derek had to admit he liked having Pete hit right after him. It meant pitchers didn't want to walk him and have to face Pete with a runner on base. Derek had done the math: Pete was the Tigers' home runs leader, but Derek was their leader in on-base percentage (OBP), stolen bases (nine for nine!), and, thanks to Pete, runs scored. But he wished he could hit homers like Pete did.

Derek's dad took him to the batting cages whenever they both had a free hour at the same time. He tried to show Derek how to add more power to his swing by putting more weight on his back foot. But it wasn't easy for Derek to change his swing and still hit the ball hard.

"You know, you might need to grow into it," his dad said. "Not everyone is built to hit a lot of home runs. You keep at it, and concentrate on solid contact. Hit the ball where it is. Remember, scoring runs is the name of the game."

Derek knew his dad was right. Still, it bothered him that he wasn't the hitting hero of the team. Even worse, he was stuck on the wrong side of the infield.

But even for Derek, winning took a lot of the sting out of his frustrations. The weak pitching of the Dodgers and Marlins had made great hitters out of all of them, and had given them a certain amount of shaky confidence—shaky because of the way they were still giving up runs.

And now here came the Tigers' biggest game of the season so far, the game that would put their confidence to its stiffest test yet.

The mighty Yankees were undefeated. They hadn't even had a close game. Two of their four victories had come via the mercy rule. From the moment they showed up at Westwood Fields that Saturday morning, their cocky confidence was obvious.

Coach Kozlowski gathered the Tigers together. "Okay, kids," he said. "Let's show these guys we're no pushovers! Let's show them we can compete, that they can't just walk all over us."

Derek frowned. In his opinion, this was no way to get the team fired up. They were out there to *win*, weren't they? Not just compete? Making it their goal to not get stomped on wasn't going to pump up anybody's confidence.

He could hear his dad's voice in his head saying, *It's the coach's decision. You just go out there and play the best you can. Don't worry about anything else.*

Looking up into the stands, Derek found his dad, mom, and sister. He waved and smiled, and they waved and smiled back. He could hear Sharlee yelling, "Go, Derek! Hit a home run!"

Jeez, Derek said to himself. Even Sharlee thought home runs were the most important thing! He went out to second base to warm up. The Yankees were up first, and Derek wondered where in the lineup his friends would be hitting.

Ryan was on the mound to start the game, with Ernesto at first. Derek, Pete, and Sims rounded out the infield, with Isaiah catching, as always.

In the outfield were Vijay in left, Mark in right, and Chris in center. Chris had become a fixture out there—a pretty good outfielder, even if his glove seemed two sizes too big for him. At least he caught the ball, or caught up with it quickly, and he had a good arm for a kid his size and weight.

Derek got into his ready position, weight forward on the balls of his feet, just like his dad had taught him. He bounced up and down a little to get loose, then settled in to wait for the first pitch.

Ryan was a fastballer, but the lefty swinger at the plate had real bat speed. He pulled Ryan's pitch right down the first baseline past Ernesto, who saw the ball go by him before he could even react. The hitter ended up on second base.

Next up was Derek's buddy Jeff from Mount Royal. Jeff pointed his bat right at Derek, sort of saying *Hello* and *We're gonna beat you* all in the same gesture.

Derek grinned and shook his head. He'd known Jeff for years, and they were friends for sure. But that didn't mean he'd forgotten that Jeff had laughed at Derek's life's dream. Far from it. Now Derek hoped he would get his chance to answer back in the best way possible—on the baseball field.

Jeff smacked a line drive in Pete's direction, but it was way over his head. In fact, it was over Vijay's head too. But Vijay didn't give up on the ball. He turned, ran, and reached up blindly, hoping against hope the ball would find his glove . . .

And it did! The Tigers erupted in cheers as Vijay held up the ball triumphantly.

Meanwhile, the runner had gone back to second base. But seeing that no one was paying attention, he made a sudden dash for third!

Derek saw him and yelled to Vijay, "THIRD! THIRD!" But Vijay couldn't hear him over the cheering and shouting. Even if he could have, he was still too amazed by the fact that he'd caught the ball to notice anything else. By the time he realized what was happening, the runner was coming home. Vijay threw the ball to Derek, but the runner beat the relay easily to make the score 1–0, Yankees.

"Wake up out there!" Pete yelled to Vijay, who looked down and kicked the ground in shame.

"Hey! The batter's up!" Derek told Pete.

"Focus on your own game," grumbled Pete as he got back into position. "What kind of a relay was that?"

There had been nothing wrong with the relay, and Derek knew it. He shook off Pete's comment and concentrated on the next play.

The next hitter up was Harry, another Mount Royal kid. Derek knew he could hit, but even he was impressed when Harry crushed a fastball deep, deep to right for an easy home run.

Jason, another friend of Derek's, was up next. He hit a triple, and Coach Kozlowski walked slowly to the mound to talk to Ryan and settle him down.

It didn't seem to help. Ryan walked the next two batters, and Coach had to come out again and make a pitching change, switching Ryan with Ernesto at first. And it was only the first inning!

But Ernesto, with his assortment of slow and slower pitches, kept the Yankee hitters off balance. They popped up twice to end the inning with the score still only 2–0.

To Derek that felt like a miracle—although the Tigers had already lost one of their two pitchers, with five innings still to go. Now it was their chance to show the Yankees that they could hit, too.

Except they couldn't. The Yankees had great pitching as

well as hitting. Jeff had told Derek he was a pitcher, but he wasn't starting today. No, he was at *shortstop.*

Jeff, shortstop for the Yankees. Pretty ironic, Derek thought bitterly. *Wearing number 13, too, just to add to the misery.*

Harry was also the Yankees' pitcher, and turned out to be the hardest thrower the Tigers had faced so far. You could barely see his pitches! Even worse, he got them over the plate more than half the time, so you couldn't just stand there and hope he would walk you.

He struck out Chris on three pitches. Derek, through sheer will and determination, fouled off what felt like a dozen pitches before finally getting an infield hit on a dribbler to third.

He stole second on a close play, but it didn't matter, because Pete struck out, and after a pair of walks to Ryan and Isaiah, Ernesto whiffed on a fastball to end the inning and the Tiger threat. Other than Derek, none of the Tigers had even made contact. Not even a foul ball.

Sheesh, thought Derek as he grabbed his mitt. *This could be a long day. . . .*

Luckily, Ernesto kept the Yankees from scoring in the top of the second. But the Tigers went down without scoring in their half of the second, with nothing more than a walk squeezed in between three more strikeouts.

Ernesto was doing fine in the third, too—until Pete made a great dive for a ball in the hole, then threw to first when he had no chance to get the runner. The ball short-hopped Ryan, hit off his shoulder, and skittered out to right field. The runner went all the way to second, then scored on a bloop single to left. The Yankees had a three-run lead, and with their pitching, Derek knew it would be hard to catch up if the Tigers gave up any more runs.

Fortunately, they didn't—at least not that inning.

Derek led off the third with a sharp single to right. It was the first hard-hit ball the Tigers had hit all day. Pete followed with a single to left, sending Derek to second.

With a 1–2 count on Ryan, Derek took off for third. The throw from the catcher beat him there, but Derek slid under the tag. "Safe!" the umpire called.

As Derek got up and began dusting himself off, he saw that somehow Pete had gotten himself in a rundown between first and second base!

Derek knew Pete should have taken off for second base the minute he'd seen Derek going for third. Clearly, he'd waited too long and now was about to be tagged out.

Derek saw an opportunity, though. Everyone's eyes were on Pete, and no one was watching him. He scooted toward home and was halfway there before the Yankees realized what was happening. Derek slid, and the umpire yelled, "SAFE!"

Pete was out, but Derek had stolen a run for the Tigers! They were back in the ball game now, down just 3–1.

That was the way it stayed until the fifth inning. Ernesto

had pitched a great game so far, saving the Tigers' bacon in the first inning and holding the Yankees to just one run since then. He had to be tired, though. Derek wondered how much longer he could keep the Yankees from scoring again.

The Tigers were down only two runs. If they could tie it up, or better yet, take the lead, it might be possible to steal this game from the mighty Yankees. Derek, leading off the fifth, knew this might be his last at bat of the day. He was determined to make the most of it.

Jeff was pitching now. Derek knew Jeff had a good arm and was always around the plate with his pitches, but Derek had faced him a million times at the Hill. Jeff's pitches were no mystery to him, so before trotting out onto the field, Derek called over Pete, Ryan, and Isaiah in the dugout to give them a quick heads-up about what they might face. Derek knew Jeff's pitches tended to tail off to the right, so that's where he swung. Not trying to hit a home run—just hitting it where it was, like his dad had told him.

CRACK! The ball went sailing over the third baseman's head and down the left field line! Derek made it to second, clapping his hands to urge his teammates on. He could hear his parents and Sharlee screaming from the stands, shouting their encouragement.

But the Tigers and their fans went quiet as Pete struck out on three straight pitches, swinging for the fences when he should have just been trying to get a base hit to keep the rally going.

Ryan then went down 0–2. Derek took off for third on the next pitch, and made it easily. He looked up just in time to see and hear the umpire call, "Strike three! Yer out!"

Two outs now. "Come on, Isaiah," Derek said under his breath. "COME ON!" he yelled, clapping his hands.

Isaiah nodded, cocking his bat. Jeff threw his best fastball, and Isaiah popped it up to short right field. The first baseman ran back to get it, and the right fielder and second baseman both came over too.

Derek knew there were two outs, so he didn't wait to see if the ball was caught. He was already standing on home plate when the ball dropped between the three of them!

"YESSS! Nice going, Isaiah!" he yelled, leaping up and down with his arms in the air. But the celebration was short-lived, as Isaiah, who'd kept on running when the ball had dropped, was caught by a good throw to second to end the inning with the score Yankees 3, Tigers 2.

The Tigers had gotten back into the game, thank goodness. But they'd just lost a great chance to tie the score!

In the top of the sixth, Jeff led off for the Yankees with a screamer over Derek's head. Derek turned and leapt as high as he could, snagging the ball in the netting of his mitt. The ball almost came out, it had been hit so hard. But Derek managed to hang on to it, and as he looked at the sno-cone sticking out of the web of his mitt, he smiled.

Derek heard Jeff yelling something at him angrily, but Derek just kept grinning. There was nothing sweeter than a little on-the-field revenge, and after waiting for six whole innings, he'd finally gotten it!

The next batter walked. After a strikeout, Derek began to breathe a little easier. One more out . . .

The runner on first tried to steal on the next pitch. The hitter grounded the ball to short. Pete moved to his right and snagged it—but instead of throwing to first for the sure out, he threw to second.

Derek was covering on the attempted steal, but the runner got in before the throw, and by the time Derek wheeled and fired to first, the man was safe there, too!

"Come on, Jeter!" Pete cried out, flapping his arms in frustration.

"*What?* What'd I do?" Derek asked.

Pete didn't answer, because really there was nothing he could say. He was the one who'd thrown to the wrong base when he'd had a sure out at first.

Derek thought he knew what had happened. Pete had forgotten how many outs there were and had been trying for a double play when there were already two outs!

He *thought* that was what had happened, but he couldn't be sure. Anyway, what was the use of talking about it? Right now they had a game that was about to get away from them. A game they had a chance to win, against the best team in the whole league!

The next hitter put all such thoughts to rest, though. He hit a long ball past Chris in center, and all three runs scored on the homer.

The Tigers came up in the bottom of the sixth, down now by four big runs. They got one runner on base when Ernesto doubled to left, but with the bottom of their order up, they didn't have much of a chance against a pitcher as good as Jeff. He mowed down Sims and Elliott. But Vijay, batting ninth, somehow got his bat on an 0–2 fastball for a dribbler down the first baseline. He beat the throw, giving himself some bragging rights back at Mount Royal, but more important, giving the Tigers some hope.

Slightly rattled, Jeff walked Chris to load the bases. Here was Derek's chance to be the hero. He knew Jeff wouldn't give him anything too good to hit, and thought he might try a fastball on the outside part of the plate. And that's what Derek got. He hit the ball on the button . . . right at the Yankees' first baseman.

It was a loss, but at least the Tigers put a scare into the Yankees. Coach was right. They did compete.

Derek stood in the line to shake hands with the Yankees. Jeff grinned as he got to Derek. "I thought you had me there."

"Well, yeah, but you guys did win the game, so . . ."

"Yeah, we did, didn't we! Oh well. Good luck from here on in."

It was the usual back-and-forth. But this time it stung a little more than Derek wanted to admit.

Derek stole a glance at Coach Kozlowski. He and a bunch of the kids were putting the equipment back into the duffel bags. Pete was not one of them. He was sitting alone on the end of the bench, pouting about the game.

Derek noticed the coach staring at his son. Coach seemed to be deep in thought, stroking his chin. Then he turned, and his gaze found Derek. Then it went back to Pete.

Hmmm . . .

Derek wondered if his own fielding feats at second, as well as Pete's poor play at shortstop (not to mention his attitude), had finally made an impression on the coach.

Nah, it was probably too much to hope for. "Do your own job," his dad had told him, "and let the coach do his."

Sighing, Derek let go of it and headed for the stands, where his family was always waiting for him with open arms, win or lose.

Chapter Ten

PARENTS AND TEACHERS

". . . and how much do you think this swanky new eight-track stereo system goes for?"

Derek and his dad were watching TV. *The Price Is Right*, to be exact. The show had become a mini-obsession for the two of them.

"Derek?"

"How should I know? I never bought a stereo system."

"Eight-track," said his dad. "It's the wave of the future."

"I don't know. . . . Two hundred dollars?"

"Okay. I say $170."

"Marci has guessed $140. And the price is . . . $175!"

"Yesss!" said Mr. Jeter.

Derek frowned. "If I had a stereo, maybe I'd know how much it cost."

"You would have one if you paid for it. Anyway, you keep playing against the best, and your game will keep improving."

That made Derek think about his team's recent loss to the Yankees. He'd improved his own personal game, without a doubt, but his team had still lost. And he couldn't remember the last time he'd beaten his dad at . . . well, at *anything*. Still, it didn't make him want to give up. It made him want to try again, and try harder.

"Hal-looooo!" came Aunt Dimp's lilting voice from the front door as the tall, smiling woman let herself in.

"Aunt Dimp!" Sharlee shrieked from upstairs. There followed the patter of little feet as she raced to the stairs and then carefully climbed down. Sharlee was still too young to take stairs at a fast pace.

"Come over here, you little sweet thing!" Aunt Dimp swept Sharlee up in her arms and spun her around, high in the air. Sharlee squealed with delight.

Aunt Dimp was Mr. Jeter's sister, and she lived not far away. Her real name was Sharlee, but everyone called her Dimp because she had big dimples on her cheeks. Besides, it was less confusing with only one person in the family called Sharlee.

In fact, Aunt Dimp was here to babysit for the *other*

Sharlee, because Derek and his parents were going to his school for parent-teacher night.

"How are you doing, Sis?"

"Just fine!" said Aunt Dimp, putting Sharlee down so she could take her coat off.

Just then the front door opened again, and Mrs. Jeter stepped inside. "Oh boy!" she chirped, as everyone hugged and kissed. "It's a family gathering."

"Come on, Jeter," said Derek's mom, not taking her jacket off. "You too, old man. We're going to be late if we don't get right on out of here."

Derek had lots of other things on his mind, but now he started to worry about what Ms. Wagner might say about him to his parents. He didn't *think* she would say anything bad—but you never knew.

Sure enough, it turned out he had every right to be worried. "Mr. and Mrs. Jeter," she said, greeting them. "Derek. Have a seat."

She checked her notes as they all sat down. "Derek is a very intelligent child," she began. "He works well with others and generally gets good grades." Derek checked to see if his parents were paying attention. He sure hoped so.

"However," his teacher went on, "he did have quite a falling-off in math on the last test. An eighty-four is not what I expect from Derek."

"Neither do we," his mom agreed.

"That won't happen again," Derek said quickly. "I promise."

"Good!" Ms. Wagner said, giving him a little smile that didn't seem that warm. "Now, there's this *other* little matter . . ."

"Oh?" His dad's face suddenly grew serious. So did his mom's as she leaned in, paying close attention.

"Derek tends to daydream in class a bit. I don't worry too much about it, because his grades are usually good. But with this last math mark . . . you see what I mean."

"Yes, we do," said his dad, looking right at Derek.

"We certainly do," said his mom, nodding slowly.

"*And* he has been getting into the habit lately of talking in class with his friends in the back row," Ms. Wagner continued. "So I decided to move the other boys up front to break them up. It seems to be working out well so far."

"Derek!" said his mom. "I'm surprised at you!" His dad only gave him a sharp look, saying nothing.

"Overall, I don't see anything to worry about," Ms. Wagner finished. "Just please be sure Derek understands that his attention is required in class at all times."

"Well, thank you, Ms. Wagner," Mr. Jeter said, getting up and shaking her hand.

"We'll make sure Derek gets the message," his mom added, giving him the eye.

"I got it!" Derek assured her. "I already got it."

"Mm-hm," said his mom, not totally sold.

"Oh, there is one other thing," Ms. Wagner suddenly said. "I nearly forgot to bring it up. But . . . well, I gave the class an assignment to write an essay about their life's dream . . . and I specifically told them to write about realistic goals."

Uh-oh. Derek could see where this was going, and his stomach felt tied up in knots.

"Well, it's sweet and all—*very* cute. But we're in third grade now, and I expect the students to have realistic responses to an essay question. Derek wrote that he wanted to be shortstop for the New York Yankees!" Ms. Wagner gave Derek's parents a meaningful look over the top of her glasses.

"Derek," said his mom. "Would you please wait outside? We'd like a moment to speak with Ms. Wagner privately."

Derek stiffened. What did they want to talk about that he wasn't allowed to hear?

"Derek," said his father. "Outside. Now."

Derek did as he was told, closing the door behind him. On the other side, he could hear a muffled voice—his mother's. But he couldn't make out what she was saying, and he knew he wasn't meant to, so he sat down on the hallway floor and leaned his back against the wall.

It took a good few minutes. Then, finally, the door opened and his mother emerged, her eyes ablaze, her mouth set. His dad followed behind her. With a nod to Ms. Wagner, he shut the door. "Let's go, Derek," he said, not stopping to wait. Derek had to catch up to them as they marched quickly down the hall.

"What was that about?" he asked them.

"We just wanted Ms. Wagner to understand that we support your dream and we encouraged her to as well," his mom said sharply. "You just stick to your dream, and keep working hard toward it. Never mind what anybody says about it being 'realistic.' It's realistic as long as you're working to make it real."

Derek followed his parents out into the cold, rainy night. He was shivering and wet, but he had never felt happier. He knew they would be all over him now, about talking in class, and daydreaming, and his disappointing math grade. He knew Ms. Wagner would be on high alert if he gave her even the smallest of excuses. (Which he was determined *never* to do again!)

He knew the odds of achieving his lifelong dream were against him. After all, what chance did he have of being the Yankees' shortstop if he couldn't even get to be short-stop on his Little League team?

But he didn't care if the odds were long. He didn't care if his teacher didn't think his dreams were realistic.

The only thing that mattered was that his parents were in his corner. They'd stuck up for him when it had mattered most! If *they* believed his dream was realistic, who was he to think otherwise?

When they got home, Derek's mother said to Aunt Dimp, "Can you stay an extra fifteen minutes with Sharlee, please? We need to talk to Derek alone."

Chapter Eleven
DRIVEN

When Derek returned to school the next day, he noticed a change in Ms. Wagner. She seemed to have gained a new respect for him.

Something about that parent-teacher conference had opened her eyes. And rereading that contract had opened his. Suddenly it was easy to pay strict attention in class.

It didn't hurt that Jeff and Gary were sitting on opposite sides of the front row, while he was still back in the last row, near the coat closets. From that quiet spot, Derek had a perfect view of the back of Gary's head, and as he stared at it, he thought, *I'm going to beat you out on the next math test. You wait and see.*

Now determined, Derek went home every day after

school and, after his regular homework, went over that day's math lesson again from beginning to end.

That same focus served him well on the ball field when it was time for the Tigers to play. But even though he was hitting above .500, the Tigers still lost two of their next three games, bringing their season record to 4–4.

Derek kept making great plays at second base, even though it pained him to hear Coach Kozlowski praise him after games, saying, "Boy, have we got a great second baseman!"

He hadn't given up on being the shortstop, but it was getting late in the season for him to keep hoping for a shot at Pete's position.

"Hey, up there. Hel-looo!"

Derek heard Vijay calling him from outside. He heard the *thwack* of the baseball as Vijay bounced it off the brick wall of the Jeters' house

Derek went to the window, opened it, and leaned out. "Hey, man. I'm trying to study math in here!"

"Never mind math! Come play baseball with me! Playing by yourself is boring! Where've you been all week?"

"Studying, I told you. I've got a math test, and I'm settling for nothing less than a hundred."

"No worries. I'll study with you tonight! Just come over after dinner. You'll see. I know all that stuff, easy. Now come on down and bring your mitt. We've still got an hour before dinner!"

"Nah. I'm gonna study now, too. But I will take you up on the offer, all right?"

"Sheesh. So serious." Vijay shook his head in wonder.

"You got that right," Derek said with a grin, closing the window and shutting out Vijay. "Got to be like a samurai," he told himself, trying to forget all thoughts of baseball for the moment. "Concentrate like a ninja . . . *kee-yah!*"

He did a few mimed "karate" moves and kicks that were more like break dancing than anything else. Then he sat back down at his desk and got to work.

After dinner Derek told his parents he was going over to study with Vijay. They gave him a disbelieving look, but he said, "No, really. He offered to help me with tomorrow's math test. See?"

He showed them the math textbook tucked under his arm, and the fact that he had no mitt, bat, or ball with him.

"Sounds good to me," said his dad.

"Go for it!" said his mom. And Derek was out the door.

Vijay's mom worked as a nurse, and Mr. Patel was one of those guys who worked the radiation machines in hospitals. But even with their crazy schedules, they still somehow made time to cook Indian food, which meant they had to shop for all the fresh and exotic ingredients. Derek had no idea where they found the time. They were always bustling around the apartment doing stuff, that was for sure.

There were lots of cool things about the Patel home. There were statues of ladies with six arms, and a painting of a blue man surrounded by blue women dancing. When the Patels played music on their stereo, it was a different kind of music that Derek knew must be from India.

The apartment always smelled wonderful, too. Spices Derek had never smelled anywhere else filled the air and made him hungry. Mrs. Patel usually tried to make him sample the dishes she'd cooked. Derek liked most of it— and on the rare occasion when he didn't, he always pretended to. He could see how much his opinion mattered to her.

The Patels treated him like royalty—maybe because he'd been Vijay's first friend after they'd moved here. Anyway, when Derek stepped through the door, there was already a plate of food at the table, and Mrs. Patel tried to get him to eat.

"Aw, no thanks," he said. "I just ate. I'm so full, I could explode!"

"At least some dessert?" she said, looking disappointed.

"Maybe later. After we study."

"Mommy, please. Derek needs to work," said Vijay. "Don't worry. I'm going to coach him, and he's going to get a one hundred."

"That's great, Vijay!" said his father, who was on the living room couch reading a newspaper that was written in a different alphabet. "Chin up, Derek. You can do it!"

"Thanks, Mr. Patel," Derek said, and followed Vijay upstairs.

"So," Vijay said. They were sitting side by side in front of Vijay's desk now, with Derek's book open to the section he had to review. "Now tell me. Why so crazy about math all of a sudden?"

Derek grinned. "The real reason? I want to beat Gary Parnell for once."

"Aaahh! Now we're talking!" Vijay rubbed his hands together eagerly as he pictured the inevitable defeat of the math king. "Where do we start?"

"It's a lot of stuff," Derek cautioned. "All the way to page 434."

"Twenty pages? Wow. Well, let's get started, eh?"

"Thanks, Vijay. I really appreciate this," Derek said. "I'm sure there are lots of other things you'd have more fun doing, so why did you offer to help out?"

"Huh? Because you're my friend!"

"Sure, but you've got tests coming up yourself. Don't you need to be working on your own stuff? I mean, I know you're a genius and everything, but—"

"Ha!" It was a joke, of course, and Vijay took it that way, although he really was very smart. Vijay would have no problem achieving his life's dream of being a great doctor, Derek thought.

"No, but really. Why are you doing this for me?" Derek asked.

"Derek, remember those times when Pete was screaming at me, telling me how bad I was?"

"Oh yeah, I remember."

"The coach didn't stick up for me. None of the other kids said anything. You were the only one who came over and stood by me."

"What did I do, though?" Derek said. "I didn't get into a fight with Pete over it, I know that."

"No, but you told *me* he was being a jerk, and not to listen to him or take it personally. If not for you, I would have just had to sit there feeling bad. So . . . you helped me out. Now I help you out, okay?"

"Okay," Derek said. "Sounds good to me."

What Derek didn't tell Vijay was that he too knew what it was like to be picked on. One time on the school bus, an older kid had called him "Oreo" because of the color of his skin. When he told his mom about it later that night, he could sense her anger, but she didn't say anything right away. He could see her searching for the right words to turn something negative into something positive. Finally, she asked him, "Do you like Oreo cookies?" When he nodded yes, she said, "Those are your favorite cookies. People love Oreos."

• • •

Derek strode into class the next day with sublime confidence. He practically glided into the room, his math book under his arm.

Gary was already there, in his new seat in the front row right by the window. He stared right at Derek.

Derek returned his stare, not taking his eyes off Gary the whole way to the back row. Neither did Gary take his eyes off Derek.

This was going to be fun.

Ms. Wagner came in carrying a sheaf of test booklets. "Okay, class. Take your seats and let's get going."

"Yeah," Derek said under his breath, watching Gary as he took his booklet from the teacher. "Let's get going."

Chapter Twelve

WINS AND LOSSES

"Hey, Derek! Can I talk to you for a minute?"

Derek stopped taking grounders at second and jogged over to where Coach Kozlowski was standing by the bench. Two things were odd about this. First, the coach had gotten Derek's name right for a change. Second, he never took the time to speak one-on-one with kids—unless he was going to *bench* them.

That couldn't be it, could it? Derek had played a pretty flawless second base so far and had set his mind on making the most of the opportunity, even if it wasn't his first choice. He was hitting a team-leading .565, although he had had only one home run. So what could the coach possibly want with him?

"Derek," said Coach Kozlowski, "I know this season hasn't been easy on you so far."

Huh? Now Derek was totally confused. Had his dad or his mom said something to the coach about Derek's hurt feelings? He sure hoped not!

Nah, he thought. *They wouldn't do that.* They'd want him to find his own way through it. But then, what was this about?

"I want to shake things up a little," the coach was saying. "So I've decided to make some changes in the infield. Pete's going to be pitching today. So I'm putting you at short."

"What!?" Derek blurted out, dumbstruck.

Now it was the coach's turn to look confused. "Funny. I thought you'd be pleased. It's where you wanted to play, isn't it?"

"Yeah!" Derek was quick to agree. "Yeah, I'm pleased, Coach. Thanks! But . . . who's going to play second?"

"Ryan. And then Pete, when I put Ryan in to pitch."

"You mean . . ."

"That's right. You're at short from now on. We need to shore up our fielding."

Neither of them said another word. They both knew what Coach was getting at. Pete had been making lots of errors at the most important position in the infield.

Coach Kozlowski had made a change to help the team win. But Derek knew it would cost the coach dearly. Pete had to be steaming mad about this!

Sure enough, he didn't look happy. Pete was standing on the mound firing fastballs so hard that his father said, "Hey, save your arm for the game." But that didn't stop Pete from trying to throw the ball right through Isaiah's catcher's mitt.

He couldn't throw a tantrum in front of everyone, of course. Besides, being made the starting pitcher wasn't exactly a demotion. The pitcher had the game in his hands, after all. Still, Pete looked far from happy, especially when he saw Derek take his position at shortstop.

The Tigers were 4–4, and if they won this game, they had a legitimate shot at the upcoming play-offs. That had to be why Coach Kozlowski had decided to make his move now. The trouble was, today they were playing the Orioles, who were in second place behind the Yankees, at 7–1. In fact, their only loss was to the Yankees, by one run.

"Those kids look huge!" said Sims, coming up alongside Derek.

"Yeah, they do," said Derek. "Wonder what they're eating."

That cracked Sims up. Then he said, "Hey, glad you're at short."

"Thanks."

"Let's make some plays, huh?"

"Yup." Derek high-fived Sims and got ready for the game to start.

It was hard to concentrate in the beginning, since he

was so excited. Here he was, at short! He could scarcely believe it. He hadn't said a word. He'd just let his play in the field speak for him, and the coach had noticed!

It was a lesson Derek promised himself he would never forget. If he'd gone to the coach and complained—or even mouthed off to his teammates about it—this would probably never have happened.

But if he'd made it to his first goal this fast, it had to be possible for him to reach higher, more difficult goals—including his ultimate dream!

Derek forced himself back into the present moment. He'd gotten here by playing well, and if he meant to stay at shortstop for the rest of the season, he had to show he could handle the job.

Pete turned out to be a pretty good pitcher. He had the strongest arm of anyone on the Tigers, for sure. His only problem was the same one he'd had that first day, when he and Derek had pitched to each other on the sidelines. Pete couldn't get it over the plate to save his life.

He struck out the first Orioles hitter, who swung at balls in the dirt and over his head. But the other Orioles, watching from the bench and the on-deck circle, quickly saw that Pete was wild. And if they hadn't noticed, their coach sure had. "Take two strikes!" he told his team, loud enough for Pete to hear.

Soon there were two men on base. Each had walked on four pitches. Coach Kozlowski paid a tense visit to his son on the mound. After that, Pete hit the next batter square in the backside.

With the bases loaded and a gigantic kid coming to the plate, Derek knew the Tigers were in trouble. He also knew that Coach couldn't come to the mound again without changing pitchers.

Derek quickly jogged to the mound, realizing that Pete needed help. "Hey," he said, ignoring the look Pete was giving him. "Don't worry about letting them swing at a strike. They can't hit you." He could have yelled at Pete and told him to throw it over the plate but he knew that wouldn't have helped. So he pretended to think Pete was throwing wild on purpose.

Pete seemed startled to get encouragement from Derek, but he didn't say anything. He just nodded, took a deep breath, and blew it out. "Go get 'em!" Derek said, clapping him on the back with his mitt and heading back to short.

Pete composed himself. He blew two fastballs right by the hitter, right down the middle of the plate.

By the third pitch, though, the hitter was ready for another fastball. Now was the time for Pete to change up and throw a slow pitch, to confuse the hitter. But Pete hadn't been practicing pitching all season, and Derek knew he probably didn't have a slow pitch.

Derek shifted a little to his left. If Pete threw a fastball, the hitter probably wouldn't be able to pull the pitch. He was more likely to hit it up the middle.

117

Sure enough, that was just what happened. The batter hit a line drive right over Pete's head. Pete ducked, but Derek reacted in a flash, running to his left and leaping to make the grab.

"THIRD! THIRD!" he heard Sims yelling.

Derek wheeled and threw to third base. The runner, having assumed that the batter had gotten a hit, was already halfway to home plate. The throw beat him back to third, and Sims applied the tag to complete the double play, ending the top of the inning with the score still 0–0!

The Tigers came over to high-five Derek and Sims as they jogged off the field, and even Pete chimed in with, "Nice going, guys."

The Tigers had dodged a bullet, but that didn't mean it was going to be an easy battle from here on in. The Orioles' pitcher had an even better fastball than Pete's, and he got it over the plate more than half the time.

He blew Chris away, but Derek had gotten a good look at those fastballs from the on-deck circle. He came to the plate ready and jumped on the first pitch to lace a liner to right.

Too bad it was straight at the right fielder for the second out. And too bad Pete struck out behind him to end the inning.

From that point on, the game was a fierce pitchers' duel. Pete seemed to have found the plate and kept his focus on throwing strikes instead of wildly trying to blow people away.

When an Orioles hitter did make contact, it was either a feeble grounder or a pop-up. Derek made a great play on a dribbler in the third, grabbing it bare-handed and firing to first across his body, nipping a very fast runner by a hair.

On the other side, the Orioles pitcher did not allow a run through the end of the fifth. Not even Derek could catch up with his blazing heater. And so the game remained scoreless going into the top of the sixth.

Pete was still on the mound. Derek was sort of surprised that Coach hadn't brought Ryan in, but not *that* surprised. Pete, after all, was mowing down the mighty Orioles like no Tigers pitcher had done to any team all season. And he hadn't looked a bit tired doing it either.

Now, though, all that throwing seemed to start taking its toll. Pete went 3–0 on the leadoff hitter before getting him on a sizzling grounder to Derek's left. Derek dove for it, snagged it in the webbing of his mitt, popped to his feet, and fired a bullet to first for the out. That made three key hits he'd stolen from the Orioles that day!

But after striking out the next hitter with bad pitches, Pete hit the following batter on the arm. Now there was a runner on first with two outs. Pete started the next hitter off with a sizzling fastball for a strike. But just as the catcher threw the ball back to Pete, the runner on first took off for second, trying to get into scoring position.

"Second base!" Derek yelled. He had seen the runner go

before anyone else. Ryan at second was caught off guard and didn't cover the base, so Derek sped over to take the throw.

Pete wheeled and fired, but he misjudged the timing, and the ball almost went into the outfield, which would have sent the runner to third at least! Luckily, Derek was able to knock the errant throw down and keep the ball near enough to hold the runner.

The count went to 1–2 on the hitter, and the next pitch was a ball. But Derek saw that the runner was trying a second time to sneak a steal on the throw back from the catcher. Quickly, Derek dashed back to the base ahead of the runner and yelled, "Pete!"

Pete, who had just caught the ball from the catcher, saw that there was daylight between Derek and the runner, and fired the ball to second. Derek was set to make the tag, and the ball got there before the runner. Unfortunately, Pete's throw was in the dirt, and the ball got by Derek and skipped into the outfield.

The runner, who had slid back into second, saw the ball get by Derek and ran for all he was worth. Vijay caught up with it and threw it in, but the Oriole runner scored easily, and the Tigers were down, 1–0.

"You idiot!" Pete yelled at Derek. "You let that throw get right by you!"

"Hey, Pete! Knock it off!"

It was the coach's voice, and Pete seemed stunned to

hear it. Derek was surprised too. Never before had Coach Kozlowski told his son to hold his tongue!

Pete kicked the dirt of the mound as his dad came out to take the ball from him and give it to Ryan. Then, to Derek's shock, Coach sent his son to the bench and brought out Elliott to play second!

Jeez! thought Derek. He had never thought he'd see that happen. He just hoped having Elliott, who'd never played in the infield, at second for one more out didn't come back to cost the Tigers.

Luckily, Ryan got the kid at bat to ground out to first, ending the inning. Now the Tigers had three outs to get a run and save their play-off hopes.

Derek grabbed a bat and was headed out to the on-deck circle when he heard Pete mutter something as he passed by. "What did you say?" Derek asked him, turning.

"I said I heard that you think you're gonna be shortstop for the New York Yankees someday."

"So?"

"You stink at shortstop, Jeter. You'll never play in the pros at any position, let alone short."

Derek had heard worse, but he still felt a wave of rage go through him, followed by another wave of doubt. Was Pete just doing a "sour grapes" thing? Or had that error really been Derek's, not Pete's?

Was he kidding himself about being the Yankees' short-stop someday? Or was he just letting somebody else's bitterness throw him off track? Derek forced himself to shake off all the negative thoughts and turn his attention back to the game.

The Orioles' starter was still pitching, and he struck out Chris for the third time that day. Then Derek came to the plate, expecting a fastball, and was amazed when he swung right through the first slow pitch of the day!

"He should have saved that for strike three," Derek muttered under his breath, getting back into the batter's box. He rapped the next pitch up the third baseline. The third baseman made an incredible play, but his throw was wild, and Derek wound up safe at first with one out.

Pete came to the plate, and Derek had a decision to make. If he tried to steal second and failed, Pete would never let him hear the end of it. On the other hand, the Tigers hadn't made much contact today. If Derek didn't get himself into scoring position, they probably had no chance to score.

Derek wanted to run on the first pitch, but that nagging sliver of doubt froze him, and he never made his move. The same thing happened on the next pitch. And then Pete hit a soft liner that the pitcher snagged. Derek found himself still at first, and now there were two outs!

He took off on the very next pitch, determined to give his team at least a shot at scoring a run. He slid in just ahead of the throw, and was about to start clapping his hands when he heard the ump say, "OUT!"

"What?" Derek couldn't believe it. "I was safe, Ump!" he pleaded. "Safe by a mile!"

"No, you weren't," the ump insisted, although Derek *knew* he'd been safe. He'd tried to get them a run and had wound up making the last out of the game!

"NO!" he shouted. "No! I was safe! Aw, man . . ."

As he made his way back to the bench, eyes on the ground, he heard Pete calling his name. "Nice work, Jeter," he said bitterly. "You just cost us our entire season."

Derek's family was waiting for him in the bleachers, and they looked concerned.

"I was *safe!*" he told them. "Did you see how badly the ump missed that play?"

His mom put a hand on his shoulder. "Never mind, old man," she said. "You played a great game against a really tough team."

"Dad, you saw it, didn't you?"

"I saw it," his dad confirmed. "Derek, I'm not the umpire, and neither are you."

"But—"

"These umpires give their time because they care about kids, and they know how good it is for kids to have a chance to play sports. Now, I know they're not perfect, and sometimes they get it wrong. It's just too bad for you that your team got a bad call today. But these things even out. The point is, the umpires deserve respect and gratitude—not arguing. Remember what we wrote in your contract? 'Respect others'? Umpires are included in that group."

"Derek," his mom said, "your father's right. I'm sure that umpire would feel bad if he knew he'd gotten the call wrong. But he's out there trying his best, just like you. And he's doing it for your benefit, not his own."

Derek hung his head and sighed. He knew they were right. But it *just wasn't fair*!

And now his team was out of the play-off picture. What had started off as a great day, with him getting his chance at shortstop, had ended in disaster, with his dreams of a championship destroyed!

Worst of all was the feeling deep down, where it mattered, that Pete was right—that it *had* been Derek's fault for not catching that pickoff throw from the mound.

Derek knew it would have been a really tough catch. But in his heart he felt he should make *every* catch, every time—and that if he didn't, it was *always* his fault.

Chapter Thirteen

CHECKMATE

"Check. Your move."

Derek stared down at the chessboard that sat in the center of the kitchen table. His white pieces were all bunched up in the corner of the board, while his father's black pieces were closing in from both the front and the side.

Derek moved his king and sighed. He rested his chin on his fists, with his elbows propping him up as he leaned forward on the table.

"You sure you want to move there?" his dad asked.

"I don't care," Derek said miserably.

"You know, it's been a while since I've seen you get this down," his father said. "You want to talk about it?"

"It's just . . . I don't know," Derek said. "If we'd won that game, we'd still be in the play-off hunt. Now it's like . . ." He fell silent, words failing him.

His dad tried to guess where Derek was going. "You know, sometimes it just doesn't work out, no matter how much you want it. Even the New York Yankees don't win the pennant every year."

"I know, but . . . I just wish we had more really good players, like the Yankees and the Orioles," Derek said, his mind still on Little League matters

"Well, that's the thing about team sports, Derek," his dad said. "You're only as good as the team you're on. That doesn't mean you can't help your teammates be the best they can be and help your team play as well as it can—*as a team*."

Mr. Jeter paused, considered the board, and moved his queen. "Of course, in individual sports, like chess, the better player almost always wins. By the way, checkmate."

Derek slumped in his chair. "I'm tired of losing!" he said, knocking some of the pieces off the table. "I hate losing, and I lose every single time! At *The Price Is Right*, at Scrabble, at chess, at basketball . . ."

"Then how come you keep coming back for more?"

That question stopped Derek cold. He had no answer for it.

"Let me help you," said his dad. "You keep coming back because you want to win so badly."

"But I never do!"

"Yes, but that doesn't make you a loser. It makes you a *winner*. Because every time you compete, you're learning and getting better. You've been coming close lately at chess—although not today. You have other things on your mind today, and I can't say I blame you."

He got up and stood beside Derek, putting a hand on his shoulder. "Anyhow, one of these days you *will* beat me, old man. And when you do, it's going to feel really, really good. You know why?"

"Why?"

"Because you'll know you earned it with hard work and patience and downright stubborn mule persistence. You keep that up, and apply it to everything you do, and you'll end up in Yankee Stadium yet."

He gave Derek's shoulder a squeeze, then said, "Don't forget to clean up in here." Then he went into the living room.

Derek picked up the pieces and put away the chess set, then went over to the sink and got busy washing the dishes. He knew his dad was right. He knew his dad was only trying to teach him a valuable lesson.

Derek could see the day coming in the future when he would beat his dad at chess, and even at basketball. Although he could never see beating him in Scrabble, or *The Price Is Right*.

He really appreciated his dad's mentioning his big

dream, too, and saying Derek could get there if he just kept on competing and coming back for more.

Still, none of that made him feel one bit better about not making the play-offs.

Derek's mom came home late, after a Parents' Association meeting at the school. Lying on his bed in the dark, Derek heard her come in and greet his dad. When their voices got quiet, he wondered what they were talking about. Probably about the little tantrum he'd thrown after getting beaten at chess, he figured.

Sure enough, he soon heard her footsteps coming up the stairs. "Derek? You awake?" she asked, knocking on the half-open door and stepping into the room.

"Hi, Mom."

"Your dad tells me there were some fireworks. You all right?"

"I guess."

She sat down on the side of his bed and ran a hand through his hair. "It'll be all right, old man. You'll feel better about things tomorrow."

"No, I won't."

"Hey, come on now," she said. "That's not my Derek talking. Don't you have three more games left in your season? What's your record now?"

"Um, 4–5?"

"Okay. So let's do some baseball math, Derek. Pay

attention now. What would the Tigers' record be if you won your next three games?"

"Uh . . . 7–5."

"And that means what?"

Derek sat up in bed, realizing that he did still have something to play for. "We'd end up with a winning record!"

"Exactly," said his mom, getting up. "I rest my case. Plus, you already accomplished one of your goals. You got to play shortstop, didn't you? So . . . I wouldn't waste another minute lying around moping. That's not going to get you anywhere. And while you're at it, why don't you try to make the All-Star team as well?"

She was right! He'd forgotten all about the All-Star game, probably because there hadn't been one in the younger leagues, and because Coach Kozlowski hadn't ever mentioned it. "Thanks, Mom!" he said, hugging her. "I never thought of it that way!"

"Derek, a loss is not really a loss if you learn something from it. It's just an important lesson on the way to your ultimate goal."

Derek grinned. The weight that had been crushing him was now totally lifted. He couldn't wait to get to Westwood Fields tomorrow.

But first there was a whole day of school to get through. Derek forced himself to pay strict attention. The school year was almost over, and he wanted to bring home a final report card that would show his parents how hard he'd worked to improve.

At the end of the day, when the bell rang, Ms. Wagner announced, "Before you leave, class, here are your math tests back. I must say, many of you did very well this time. I'm pleased. You've earned your summer break."

That brought a round of cheers from the class.

"Now, now," she said as she gave out the tests. "Don't get too excited. You've still got one more week of school, including a math final."

"Another ninety-seven!" Gary crowed, turning toward Derek and waving his test in the air. "Five in a row!"

Derek swallowed hard and lifted up the cover of his test booklet to see his grade. "*Yes!*" he cried.

He showed Gary the big red 100, underlined three times and with three exclamation points. "VERY GOOD, DEREK!" was written under it.

"WHAT!" Gary's brow furrowed, and he walked right over to Derek to see. "Well, that's just . . . that's just dumb luck!" he sputtered. "What did you do, copy from somebody else's test?"

"No way! I work hard for my grades," Derek shot back. "Do you?"

"Huh? Of course not! I don't need to!"

"Well, I don't know about that, Gary," Derek said calmly. "Maybe you'd better start working harder."

"What!" Gary said again. "This is . . . this is . . . this is a once-in-a-lifetime event It'll never happen again, not in a million years!"

Derek smiled as he stuffed his books into his book bag. He knew it wasn't dumb luck or the only time it would happen. He'd studied his heart out, with some help from Vijay, while Gary had taken it for granted that he'd do well on the test—and get his usual grade.

As Derek left the class, he saw that Gary was still there, sitting at his desk with a math book open to that day's chapter, studying furiously.

Ha! Derek thought. *He's already trying to get a leg up on me for the final exam!*

That didn't bother him. If Derek's beating him on the math test made Gary a better student, that was okay with Derek. At least he'd proved that Gary wasn't invincible.

Even more important, if hard work had paid off in math, it surely would pay off in baseball, too!

Chapter Fourteen

WINNERS

Not only did the Tigers win that day, by a crushing score of 9–1, but they won their next game too, 8–0, to go 6–5 on the season with one game left to go.

Pete had figured out how to throw his fastball so it stayed over the plate. He was hitting for power too. Derek was actually starting to feel good about having him as a teammate. In fact, he was starting to feel good about the whole season.

Among other things, Derek had learned not to challenge the umps. Instead, he made sure to thank them at the start of every game for volunteering their time to help kids. Getting those umpires to smile was worth the effort, Derek thought. They didn't smile much when coaches and parents were yelling at them and calling them blind. Or worse—one time the local police had to be called when a parent wouldn't stop arguing with an umpire after a controversial call.

In the field, Derek had been a standout, but he hadn't been the only one. The Tigers had finally gotten their act together as a team—too late to make the play-offs, of course. But they still had this one chance, this one game, to get revenge on the Yankees *and* finish the season as winners!

"Hey, Derek. Hey, Vijay." Jeff came over to the Tigers' bench and high-fived both of his friends. "You guys ready to lose?"

"We're not going to lose!" Vijay said, putting an arm around Derek's shoulder. "Derek's going to hit three home runs, so ha!"

"Stop," Derek said, laughing.

"No, but you'll see, Jeff. You guys are ready for a fall. Guaranteed."

"Vijay!" Derek said. "We don't need to give these guys any more motivation, huh?"

"Oh, sorry," said Vijay, but Derek could tell he really wasn't.

"Doesn't matter," said Jeff. "We're motivated anyway. If—no, when—we beat you, we go undefeated for the season."

"I knew you were going to bring that up," said Derek.

"You would too if you guys had a team like ours. Well, catch you later. I won't say 'Good luck,' because this one's not gonna be a matter of luck."

"Later," said Derek and Vijay.

After Jeff had gone, Derek turned to his friend and said, "Why'd you have to go and say that? Now I've got to hit three home runs!"

"You'll do it!" Vijay said.

"What makes you think so?"

"Because I said it, and you don't want to be embarrassed, that's why!"

"*Sheesh*. Didn't anybody ever tell you this was a team sport?"

The Tigers came to bat first. Chris, their leadoff man, had become an expert at getting walks. Then he would use his speed to drive the pitchers crazy, stealing bases whenever he had the chance. But with Jeff pitching, there was no chance of walking. Jeff was accurate as well as strong. Chris went down swinging at three straight strikes.

As Derek stood waiting in the on-deck circle, he was glad it was Jeff pitching instead of Harry. Nobody had done much with Harry's fastball last time and Derek knew Jeff's pitches from their many games at the Hill in Mount Royal Townhouses.

Jeff loved to throw pitches at different speeds, to make the hitter guess what was coming. Obviously this had worked for him all year, since the Yankees had so far gone undefeated.

Derek, though, knew how Jeff thought, and he knew that

Jeff knew that he knew. So it was a guessing game from the first. But Derek decided, before he even saw a pitch, that he would not swing at anything except a fastball.

The first three pitches came in slow, and two of them were off the plate. With the count at 2–1, Derek guessed Jeff would turn to his fastball. because that would make it easier to throw a strike. The fastball came, and Derek was ready. Knowing it would ride in on him like all of Jeff's pitches, Derek pulled his hands in and swung "inside out," lashing the ball down the first baseline!

He knew he could make it to second base safely. But Vijay had put big ideas into his head, and he decided to pull a surprise. By the time the ball came back into second, Derek was already on his way to third!

The Yankees' second baseman panicked and threw wildly, and Derek came around to score the game's first run!

"You see!" Vijay said excitedly as he greeted Derek's return to the bench. "I told you! Three home runs, man! No doubt about it!"

"That was a double and a two-base error," Derek corrected him. "Don't be calling that a homer."

"Who cares?" Vijay said. "We're winning, right? We're going to beat those Yankees! Hooray!"

It was too bad the rest of the Tigers didn't know Jeff's stuff as well as Derek did. The pitcher struck out the next two Tigers looking.

Still, the Tigers had the lead, and Pete was on the mound, firing bullets. Derek felt pretty good about their chances. Sure enough, Pete kept the Yankees off the bases for three straight innings.

The Tigers weren't hitting much either. When Derek came up to the plate again, he was leading off the fourth inning. Half the game had gone by, and it was only his second at bat!

This time Derek decided to take a different approach. He would let any fastballs go by, and wait for a nice, fat, slow pitch to clobber as hard as he could. He set his weight heavily on his back foot, the way his dad had showed him, loading up for a mighty swing. . . .

The first two pitches were fastballs for strikes. Jeff cracked a smile, thinking he had Derek set up for the changeup. Here it came. . . .

Derek hit it solidly on the sweet spot of the bat. The ball went high and deep to left center, and the two outfielders raced after it. With both of them calling for the ball, it fell right between them!

Derek was already rounding second. There was no stopping him. He sped around third without slowing down and barreled home just ahead of the throw!

"Now, *that* was a real home run!" Vijay crowed, high-fiving him along with the rest of his teammates. "Two down. One more to go!"

"Stop," Derek said, but his smile showed how pleased

he felt to be setting the example for the rest of his team. "Come on, you guys! Pick a pitch you want and just sit on it. Let's jump on these guys now!"

Pete had been listening, it seemed. He let two slow pitches go by, then cracked a fastball so far that he came home before the center fielder caught up with the ball! Ryan followed that up with a triple off a slow pitch. The Yankees' coach had seen enough. He came out and made the switch at pitcher, bringing Harry in to replace Jeff.

From then on, it was all fastballs all the time, and the Tigers couldn't seem to catch up with them. The rally fizzled, and they had to settle for a 3–0 lead.

In the bottom of the fourth, Pete walked the leadoff batter, then hit the next batter. Derek could feel the anxiety rise inside him as their lead was threatened. Two on and nobody out for Harry, who Derek knew could hit the ball a mile.

Derek trotted over to the mound. "I know this kid," he told Pete. "Keep the ball up high. He likes to hit the low ball."

"I know what I'm doing," Pete shot back. "Get back to your position." After all this time, Derek could tell that Pete still hadn't gotten over losing the shortstop job. He didn't like getting advice from the kid who'd taken his position from him, that was for sure. Derek backed off, hoping Pete would take his advice even though he resented it.

On the first pitch Pete threw one down in the dirt. Derek

wanted to call out, "Keep it high," but he knew Pete was throwing low on purpose, just to spite him.

The next pitch was low too, but not too low to swing at. Harry golfed it high and deep, and Norman, out in right field, had no chance. He caught up to it, but the sun blinded him, and he wound up using his glove to protect his face instead of trying to catch the ball.

"NOOO!" Pete moaned.

"Yesss!" Harry raised his fist in triumph as he rounded second base.

"This team stinks," Derek heard Pete mutter as he kicked the dirt in frustration.

Derek felt like saying, "If you had taken my advice, it wouldn't have happened." But he didn't. He knew the play wasn't over yet. He still had time to make something good happen.

Norman had picked up the ball and thrown it in. Derek cut the ball off, and saw that Harry had slowed down rounding third so he could showboat on his victory run home.

Derek fired the ball in to Isaiah, a perfect throw that nailed the stunned Harry at the plate! "Yer out!" the umpire shouted.

Harry fell to his knees and grabbed his head with both hands. Now it was his turn to shout "NOOO!" and Pete's turn to yell "Yesss!"

The Tigers still had the lead, thanks to Norman, Derek, and Isaiah's teamwork on the play. Derek could see his parents and Sharlee in the stands, whooping it up and shaking their raised fists in the air. Even Pete gave him a nod and pointed to Derek with his mitt.

Pete and the Tigers managed to escape the inning without any more damage, but their lead was now a shaky 3–2, with two innings still to play.

Pete shifted to second base for the rest of the game, with Ryan coming in to pitch and Ernesto moving from second to first.

In the bottom of the fifth, the Yankees mounted a rally. Derek felt sick to his stomach as he watched hitter after hitter reach base. They were clobbering Ryan's pitches, and Coach Kozlowski had to come out and make a switch, bringing Ernesto in to pitch for the first time in the last four games.

The bases were loaded with one out. Ernesto got Harry to pop up to short, and Derek cradled the ball in his glove for the second out.

That brought Jason to the plate. Ernesto threw him his best fastball, and Jason hit a grounder past the mound. Derek raced to dive for it, but it was too far away and bounced into center field. Two runs scored, and the Yankees took the lead for the first time in the game!

Derek felt like he'd been punched in the gut. They were down by a run now, with the Yankees still hitting, and just one more turn at bat to mount a comeback!

The hitter took a fastball deep to left, where Vijay was playing.

"Oh no," Derek heard Pete moan.

Derek saw that Vijay didn't know how hard the ball had been hit. "Deep, Vijay! Deep!" he yelled, hoping Vijay could hear him above everyone's screaming.

Vijay seemed to get the message. He ran back and back, then turned, sticking his glove up in desperate hope that it would find the ball . . .

And it did!

"Yeah!" Derek said, raising a fist in triumph.

"He caught it!" Pete exulted. "I can't believe it!"

"He's got some game," Derek told him. "That's the second great catch he's made this year. Give him some credit."

Pete laughed. "Yeah, right. Just dumb luck, if you ask me."

Derek knew it had been more than that, though. When the same thing had happened to Norman, he'd ducked. Vijay had at least tried—and when you try, Derek knew, you have at least a chance to succeed.

Now it was last licks for the Tigers. Derek came to the plate to lead off the top of the sixth.

Harry threw him a wicked fastball. Derek, knowing that what his team needed most was a base runner, just stuck his bat out and flicked the ball over the second baseman's head into right field for a single.

Derek looked for a chance to steal, but on the first pitch Pete made solid contact, turning Harry's fastball around and sending it way over the left fielder's head!

Derek wasted no time in rounding the bases and scoring the tying run. Pete, who wasn't very fast, came barreling around third behind him.

"Slide! Slide!" Derek yelled, motioning for Pete to get down.

This time Pete took his advice and slid. "Safe!" the umpire called. And just like that the Tigers had the lead!

Now it was the Yankees' turn for last licks. But their confidence seemed shaken, and there was a definite note of desperation as they urged their hitters on.

Ernesto got the first batter to pop up to third, and Sims put the ball away for the out. Next came a strikeout, followed by two walks.

Harry came to the plate, spat on his hands and rubbed them together, then waved his bat at Ernesto. "Come on," he said, "let's see what you've got."

Derek knew Harry, and he knew what his old friend was up to. He trotted to the mound again, and whispered to Ernesto, "He's trying to get you mad so you'll throw him a fastball. Don't do it. Act like you're going to, though. Then give him the slow change instead."

Ernesto nodded, understanding, and Derek went back to short. The pitch came in, impossibly slow, arcing high and dropping down as Harry took a mighty hack, and hit a weak dribbler to the mound. Ernesto grabbed it before Harry even got out of the batter's box. He was too busy groaning in frustration. Ernesto took a second to point at

Derek, thanking him for the good advice. Then he threw to first, and the ball game was over! The Tigers had beaten the mighty Yankees!

It was all Coach Kozlowski could do to get the Tigers' attention and line them up to shake hands with the humbled Yankees, who were still going to the play-offs but were no longer undefeated.

Derek, Pete, and the others were as excited as if they'd won the league championship. Harry, Jeff, and Jason looked like they were the ones who hadn't made the play-offs.

"Good game."

"Good game."

"Good game." It was the same phrase, repeated over and over again by each of them in turn.

But when Jeff shook hands with Derek, he said, "Good game, dude. Really, really good game."

"Hey, thanks," said Derek. "Good luck in the play-offs, man."

"Yeah. Thanks."

What was that clause in his contract? "Surround yourself with positive friends with strong values." As different as Jeff and Vijay were, Derek was proud that they were his friends.

When the handshake line was over, Derek ran over to the stands to hug his mom, dad, and Sharlee. "You guys did great!" his dad said, beaming with pride. "And you played a whale of a game, old man. A whale of a game!"

"Way to go, Derek!" his mom said, giving him a fierce hug and a kiss. "You made us all proud."

"Aw, Mom . . ."

Sharlee leapt into his arms. "Yay, Derek!" she cried.

"Hey, Derek!" It was Coach Kozlowski, calling him over to join the rest of the team. They had all gathered around the bench so he could talk to them one last time.

"I just want to say thanks to each and every one of you," the coach began. "This has been a great season, and I'm really proud of the way you guys rallied to finish with a winning record. I wish we could have gotten to the play-offs, but that's how it goes sometimes. Maybe if I'd been a better coach—"

"You were a great coach!" Isaiah said. And everyone cheered, chanting "Coach! Coach! Coach!" until he stopped them.

"Thanks, guys," he said. "Really. I'm deeply grateful. I did the best I could, and so did you. And now I want to announce my two All-Star selections."

Derek felt a pulse of excitement go through him. He leaned in, holding his breath.

"I wish I could have nominated one or two more of you, who were certainly deserving of the honor. But I get only two picks. So here they are. . . . Pete Kozlowski . . ."

Everyone cheered Pete, and he high-fived all the kids

who were within reach. Pete might not have been the nicest kid Derek had ever met, and he certainly wasn't the most popular member of the team, but even Derek had to admit he'd been the savior of their pitching staff. And he'd hit the most home runs of anyone on the team too. That had to count for something.

"And . . . ," Coach continued.

Derek held his breath again. He felt in his heart that he deserved it, but Isaiah and Ryan had also been key for the team.

". . . Derek Jeter!"

"Thanks!" Derek cried, clenching his fist and then exchanging high fives. Everyone congratulated Derek and seemed glad that he'd been named. Especially Vijay, who was beside himself with joy.

"You deserve it!" he cried, clapping Derek on the back again and again.

"Stop," Derek said, but he couldn't help smiling.

The coach raised his voice so he could be heard over the cheering. "One more thing before I treat you all to ice cream at Talbot's—"

That brought the biggest cheer yet from the team. They were all hot and sweaty, and in the mood for a celebration.

"I want to give out this trophy." He pulled it from his backpack, a beautiful gold trophy on a black marble base, of a hitter in midswing. "This," said the coach, "is for our most valuable player."

A wave of murmuring rose from the team as they exchanged guesses as to who it might be. "You'll win!" Vijay whispered to Derek. "It has to be you!"

"Come on, man," Derek said. "Don't be so sure."

"As I said," the coach went on, "lots of you made big contributions—and this was a hard decision. But in the end the choice was clear. Let's all give a big hand for our own MVP . . . *Pete Kozlowski*!"

There was a round of applause and some cheers, but they seemed halfhearted next to the ones for the coach and his All-Star selections, and especially for ice cream. Clearly the coach's choice of his own son as MVP was not nearly as popular.

"That is so *wrong*!" Vijay whispered to Derek. "You should have won!"

"Hey, he played great for us," Derek said. Inside, though, he was a little disappointed. But then he remembered the last rule: "Work hard." He knew he had done that.

"Okay. We'll all meet at Talbot's in ten minutes!" said the coach, and he began packing up their equipment for the last time.

Derek and Vijay stayed behind to help him. When they were done, Derek clapped his friend on the back and said, "Come on, Vijay. Let's go get us some ice cream and celebrate a winning season!"

Chapter Fifteen
FIELD OF DREAMS

"OW!"

"You okay, Grandma?" Derek asked, suddenly concerned. His grandmother was shaking out her glove hand.

"I'll be fine if my hand isn't broken," she answered with a smile, still wincing. "Where'd you learn to throw that hard? Seems to me that last summer you weren't throwing nearly as fast."

Derek beamed. "I'm three inches taller, too!"

"Well, now, is that right?" she said, looking impressed. After putting her mitt back on, she threw the ball back to him. She had a pretty good arm herself, Derek thought.

"Did Mom and Dad tell you I made the All-Star team?" His parents had left just an hour before, heading back to

Kalamazoo after driving Derek and Sharlee to New Jersey to spend the summer with their grandparents.

It was only eight in the morning, but Mr. and Mrs. Jeter had wanted to get an early start on their long drive home. Sharlee had woken up to kiss them good-bye, and now she was playing in the big backyard behind the house, kicking a soccer ball around with two of the neighbor children.

Their grandfather was already at work. He was the caretaker for a big church that had its own school, so he had to wake up at four thirty every morning to get to work on time. He didn't get home till seven or eight at night either.

Derek and Sharlee loved spending the summers here. It was all play, all day, with lots of sports activities and swimming in the lake whenever they wanted to cool off.

Their grandma was a huge New York Yankees fan, too. That was how Derek had come to root for the winningest team in baseball history. Even her car had a Yankees bumper sticker on it. "So," she said, "how'd your team do this year?"

"We had a winning record," Derek said proudly. "And I hit .597 for the season!"

"Hey, that's pretty good!" she said. "Even better than last year, right?"

"Yup. I didn't win the team MVP, though," he admitted.

"Oh, no? Who did, then?"

"This other kid."

Derek decided not to tell her about Pete being the coach's son. Even though Derek suspected Coach Kozlowski gave him the award to avoid a long summer, he had to admit that Pete played well enough to deserve it. "I was the MVP of the All-Star game, though. I got three hits!"

"Fantastic!" said his grandma. "See if you can catch this one, Mr. All-Star MVP!" She threw a high fly ball that Derek had to run back to grab. "Nice play!" she said, clapping her hand against her mitt.

When Derek trotted back toward her, he saw that she'd gone to the front porch and was fishing for something in her big handbag. "I've got something for you," she told him. "I know you've set your sights on being the Yankees' shortstop someday, so I've decided to do something to help make your dream come true."

"Huh?"

"First of all, if you're going to play for the Yanks, you've got to have a Yankees cap." She took a brand-new one out of her bag and handed it to him.

"Thanks, Grandma!" Derek said, giving her a hug before putting the hat on and bending the brim to break it in.

"A little birdie told me your old one had gotten too small."

"And too smelly!" Derek added with a laugh.

"They are washable, you know," his grandma said with a laugh. "AND . . ." She fished something else out of her bag, something small that she now hid behind her back.

"Second of all, IF you're going to be the Yankees' short-stop someday, you'd better watch how it's done *today*." She showed him what was behind her back.

"Yankees tickets!" Derek cried. "Wow! When are they for?"

"Tonight!" she said, pointing at the printing on the tickets. "Your grandpa's coming home early to be with Sharlee, and you and I are going to the big ballpark in the Bronx. Look there. We're sitting right behind the Yankees' dugout, so don't forget to bring your mitt. You might catch a foul ball."

"Grandma, that's so fantastic! Thank you, thank you, thank you! I love you soooo much!"

"Oh, I see. Get him Yankees tickets and he's yours forever."

"Grandma, you know that's not true!" He gave her another big hug. "You're the best ever, tickets or no tickets!"

"Okay, okay," she said. "Besides, your parents told me it was part of some contract you signed."

At seven o'clock that evening, Derek and his grandmother walked down the ramp and emerged to see the vast, green pasture of Yankee Stadium. The stadium cast its magic spell over him, same as it had done the very first time he'd seen it.

Everywhere he looked, he was surrounded by wonder.

The enormous crowd, already getting loud . . . the monuments to Yankees greats in center field . . . the cool facade that surrounded the top of the stadium . . . the lights on the roof making the grass impossibly green.

Best of all, there were the Yankees themselves, out on the field! Derek spotted Dave Winfield in right, tossing the ball around with the other outfielders. Closer in, Willie Randolph, the second baseman, was doing wind sprints to warm up.

The air was warm and smelled of hot dogs and cotton candy. His grandma bought hot dogs and sodas, and they took their seats to watch the Yankees play the Boston Red Sox.

As he sat there, taking it all in, Derek thought about the past few months that had led him here. So much had happened!

In school he'd finished with all As and Bs, just as he had agreed in his contract. Even better, he'd beaten Gary on a math test for the first time—but not the last, he promised himself.

On the Little League field, he'd helped his team win its last three games to finish above .500. He'd had a great season personally, too—getting to play shortstop and being named an All-Star. He'd even been named MVP of the All-Star game, although not of his own team.

Most important, his dream of playing for the Yankees had taken shape, his parents had promised to help him make it come true, and with his first contract signed, he would be well prepared for his negotiations with the Yankees down the road.

And now he had the whole summer to work on his game, to dream of the future, and to plot the next steps on his way to get there.

Watching the real Yankees out on the field, Derek felt full of hope and inspiration. People could say what they wanted about his dream of playing in the majors, but he didn't care. Setting his goals high had really paid off for him so far—and from here on in, the sky was the limit!

TIGERS' OPENING DAY ROSTER

Chris Chang—CF

Derek Jeter—2B

Pete Kozlowski—SS

Ryan McDonough—1B

Isaiah Martin—C

Ernesto Alvarez—P

Sims Osborne Jr.—3B

Elliott Koppel—LF

Norman Nelson—RF

Reserves: Vijay Patel, Sun Lee, Mark Feinberg

Coach: Hank Kozlowski

THE CONTRACT

Jeter Publishing's first middle-grade book is inspired by the childhood of Derek Jeter, who grew up playing baseball.

The middle-grade series will include ten books based on the principles of Jeter's Turn 2 Foundation.

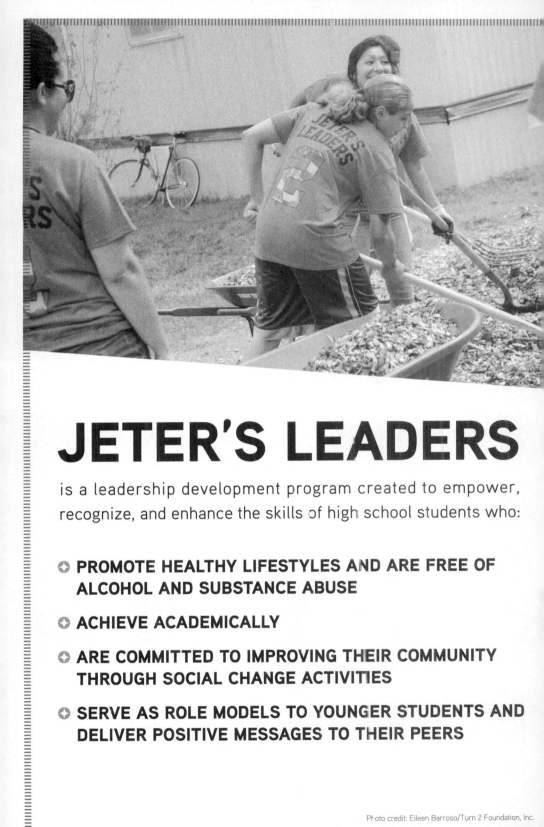

JETER'S LEADERS

is a leadership development program created to empower, recognize, and enhance the skills of high school students who:

- **PROMOTE HEALTHY LIFESTYLES AND ARE FREE OF ALCOHOL AND SUBSTANCE ABUSE**

- **ACHIEVE ACADEMICALLY**

- **ARE COMMITTED TO IMPROVING THEIR COMMUNITY THROUGH SOCIAL CHANGE ACTIVITIES**

- **SERVE AS ROLE MODELS TO YOUNGER STUDENTS AND DELIVER POSITIVE MESSAGES TO THEIR PEERS**

Photo credit: Eileen Barroso/Turn 2 Foundation, Inc.

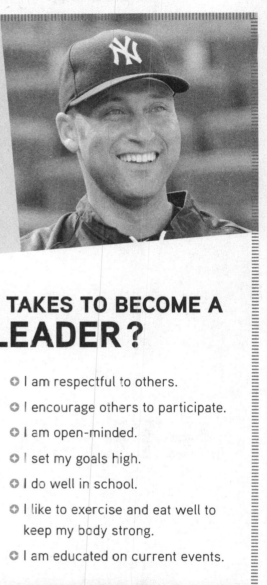

"Your role models should teach you, inspire you, criticize you, and give you structure. My parents did all of these things with their contracts. They tackled every subject. There was nothing we didn't discuss. I didn't love every aspect of it, but I was mature enough to understand that almost everything they talked about made sense." —DEREK JETER

DO YOU HAVE WHAT IT TAKES TO BECOME A
JETER'S LEADER?

- I am drug and alcohol free.
- I volunteer in my community.
- I am good to the environment.
- I am a role model for kids.
- I do not use the word "can't."
- I am a role model for my peers and younger kids.
- I stand up for what's right.

- I am respectful to others.
- I encourage others to participate.
- I am open-minded.
- I set my goals high.
- I do well in school.
- I like to exercise and eat well to keep my body strong.
- I am educated on current events.

CREATE A CONTRACT

What are your goals?

Sit down with your parents or an adult mentor to create your own contract to help you take the first step toward achieving your dreams.

For more information on JETER'S LEADERS, visit
TURN2FOUNDATION.ORG

About the Authors

DEREK JETER has played Major League Baseball for the New York Yankees for twenty seasons and is a five-time World Series champion. He is a true legend in professional sports and a role model for young people on and off the field and through his work in the community with his Turn 2 Foundation. For more information, visit Turn2Foundation.org.

Derek was born in New Jersey and moved to Kalamazoo, Michigan, when he was four. There he often attended Detroit Tigers games with his family, but the New York Yankees were always his favorite team, and he never stopped dreaming of playing for them.

PAUL MANTELL is the author of more than one hundred books for young readers.